PIRATES OF MARAUDA

Book 3:
THE INHERITANCE

by

FOREST FOX

Cover Art by

Eli D'Elia

FOREST FOX PRESS

Edited by Paul Weisser, PhD
Berkeley, California

Published by Forest Fox Press
Post Office Box 5694
Vallejo, CA 94591

info@forestfoxpress.com
www.forestfoxpress.com

Any similarity to reality is purely intentional.

This book is dedicated with fond respect and appreciation to all who helped me, too many to list here. You know who you are.

I

As the *USS Vallejo* sliced through moderate seas, dawn was breaking over the hoary Atlantic. Radioman Barrett was jolted out of his reverie when the alarm signaling an urgent message came across his panel.

The sailor snapped into action. "Con, Radio! We are receiving flash traffic..., an emergency action message. Recommend Alert One..., Alert One!"

The men of the *USS Vallejo* and her sister ship, the *California*, responded at once to the alarm. The orders from Central Command were concise.

"Those coordinates, Captain," asked Barrett," is that where I think it is?"

Ignoring the question, the commander of the underwater demolition team said, "Send word to the *California*..., we're to set course for these coordinates, best possible speed. We need to cover six hundred and forty miles."

Both anti-sub class frigates proceeded at flank speed. Neither

Barrett nor the captain wanted to say aloud that their orders were sailing them straight for the Bermuda Triangle.

Not only did Bob and his sons have the undeniable pictures they had taken of an alien craft under water, but they also had a fantastic experience that they had been completely unaware of until discovering it through hypnosis. After assessing the situation, their family physician, Dr. David Abblett, suggested that they send the file of their discovery to his brother in Washington, who just happened to be the nation's top oceanographer.

Having such an inside track to the powers that be made the whole idea of actually recovering their find seem possible. However, as the weeks that followed the doctor's report to Washington passed by without any response, Bob, Eli, and Zoe grew frustrated, insisting that Dr. Dave solicit some kind of response about their project from his brother. A week later, a brief note arrived from the master oceanographer, saying that the matter was being scrutinized, and thanking them for their "input."

"It's as if we sent in a dead fish for testing," was all Bob said when the boys read him the message.

A few days after that dismal brush off from Washington, the networks were broadcasting stories about a classified operation that had been discovered by not one, but at least six, other nations. In the days that followed, the media focused on the accusation that France had stolen the information and had sold it to the highest bidders. As fervor grew over the greed of the French, contradictory stories came out, claiming that France and the other nations had merely found the information on the Internet, where it had been temporarily misposted.

After a full week of news stories that described the tensions and ramifications of the U.S. losing control of a secret project, no one had ever mentioned what the jeopardized project was about. Of course, this could not go on, and it soon became evident that whatever the secret was, it was happening at sea.

The phone was on its third ring. The next one would switch over to the answering machine, and the moment of excitement would be gone but not forgotten.

Eli pleaded into the receiver, "Come on, pick it up!"

Zoe answered just in the nick of time.

"Hello?"

"Zoe, turn on the news…, hurry!"

"Okay. What channel?"

"*Any* channel! Is Dad there?"

"Yeah, he's right here."

"I'm coming over!"

"What's up?" Bob asked.

"I don't know," said Zoe. "Something on the news."

As Bob turned on the network news, the anchor was

recapping the current events about what seemed to be the usual international mishmash of the times.

"What about it?" Bob asked.

The scene suddenly changed to a correspondent standing on the weather deck of the *USS Newport News*, shouting into his microphone.

"We're proceeding at flank speed," said the correspondent, "to a location in the Atlantic known as the Bermuda Triangle. We have new information indicating the discovery of a UFO believed to be submerged two hundred feet below the surface."

Stunned, Bob and Zoe were still staring at the screen midway through the cat food commercial.

The incredible story of the submerged alien craft swept the globe, kindling an unprecedented wave of interest as an international race ensued to possess the prize that promised unimaginable revelations.

Bob, Zoe, and Eli were crushed to realize that they were helpless to do anything but watch as their discovery was being wrenched from them.

Within seventy-two hours of first receiving the submission from his brother, master oceanographer Dr. Brendan Abblett personally pushed his assessment and recommendations through channels to expedite their journey to the Joint Chiefs of Staff. Within two days of that meeting, there were two navy frigates hovering over the coordinates with six underwater demolition teams scouring the sea floor in search of the prize.

The leak of the classified report was a handicap the U.S.

would have to contend with. As it turned out, only the pictures, the coordinates, and some comments had actually been discovered by the rest of the world. The missing link—the part of the puzzle that contained the account of the deeds and events that went with the pictures—still remained in the sole possession of the U.S. The evidence demanded that the government spare no expenditure to retrieve what could be the most important artifact of civilization—the craft that brought the first humans to Earth.

The daily news continued to be dominated by unprecedented interest in the flying saucer and the efforts to recover it. While facts were sparse, the media made the most of what they had as extravagant hours of discussion and speculation flowed out over the airwaves.

Bob had had enough. The frustration of being ignored day after day had pushed him beyond his breaking point.

"Let's bring the whole thing to the newspapers," he said. "Maybe they'll be interested in *our* version of why everyone is rushing out to the middle of the Atlantic."

Ever since Dr. Dave had sent their file to his brother, Bob and the boys had been hoping against hope that the phone would ring and they would be included in the effort to locate and raise their discovery.

The media frenzy gave them a new grip on their position in all this, so they agreed that Bob's idea would be their next plan of action. Armed with copies of their complete file from Dr. Dave, together with their irrefutable photos, they started for the front door, when suddenly the doorbell rang.

Looking out the window, Bob gasped, "*Jee*-zus!" with that unmistakable look on his face that always accompanied his word for alarm.

It was obvious from the black unmarked car blocking the driveway that they were being called on by the Feds. The government license plates confirmed it.

The taller of the two trim six-footers in blue suits began to speak as soon as Bob opened the door.

"Good morning, gentlemen," said the suit. "Allow me to introduce ourselves. This is Special Agent Brock, and I'm Special Agent Hess. We're here in regards to your correspondence with Doctor Abblett of the Oceanographic Institute."

At a loss for words, Zoe and Eli stood frozen, amazed that they were finally being acknowledged. Bob simply glanced at the men's credentials and invited them in. The tension of the moment dissipated as everyone sat down around the kitchen table.

"As you can see," Hess began, "this discovery of yours has already ignited an international effort to possess whatever it is you found. While it's true that things got out of hand because of our own misposting of the information, it's also true that all of the other countries only have *some* of the crucial facts. Your file, the reports from your family doctor containing the fantastic story of your alleged experiences, remains top secret."

At the words *top secret*, Bob, Eli, and Zoe looked like the cat that had swallowed the canary.

Hess took a breath while they digested what he was telling

them. Then he continued, "Please understand that because your records are now classified, any disclosure of them will result in severe penalties. This, of course, means you must never mention your relationship to any of this."

Agent Hess's crushing statement had a numbing effect on the trio as they considered the potential trouble they might already be in for sharing the pictures and story with friends.

"When the time is appropriate," said Hess, "rest assured that the government has every intention of making a formal acknowledgment of your contribution."

This conciliatory afterthought hardly cushioned the foreboding shock Hess had instilled in his listeners.

After making his official statement, Hess had nothing more to say.

"I guess you're gonna want *these*, then," Bob said, pushing his copy of the file across the table.

Agent Brock gathered up the papers, and both men quickly took their leave.

The trio watched out the window as the black car drove off.

Bob was the first to speak: "Another five minutes, and they would've missed us. That was a lucky piece of timing for them, I'd say."

Zoe, who was thoroughly annoyed, looked over at Eli with a sarcastic grin. "Yeah, great timing or *something*," he said. "More likely, *something*. They're not known for their intuition."

"You think they're watching us?" Bob asked. "Maybe they've got the place bugged!" He was more serious than melodramatic.

"With or without any records," Eli said, "there isn't much we can do about anything anyway. It's out of our hands.... And good riddance, I say!"

"That's our find out there, and we're letting it get away!" Zoe said, totally frustrated.

"Yeah, I know," Bob said. "But there's nothing we can do about it!"

The next international competitor to arrive over the site were the French, with two nuclear cruisers, a tactical carrier, and the *Napoleon*, their state-of-the-art deep sea rescue vehicle (DSRV). The U.S. now had eight large ships of various designations, in addition to the underwater demolition teams, which had been on the scene even before the story broke.

The divers had had more than enough time to scour the entire area's sandy bottom before the international community began to arrive. After their inclusive scan, it became obvious that the craft pictured in the not so top-secret photos was nowhere to be found, leaving only two possibilities: either the mysterious craft had taken off, or it had somehow slipped over the edge of the newly formed sea cliff into the boundless abyss. This latter scenario was most likely, given the several undersea quakes that had rocked the area since the pictures were taken almost a year before.

Even with the grim prospect of undertaking an abyssal

search, the U.S. remained undaunted in its intention to retrieve the prize. While the American team waited for the newly commissioned super-DSRV *Trieste III* to be delivered to the scene, they mapped out their plans for a search that promised to test all of the latest equipment to the limits.

The Navy divers were kept busy going back and forth from their underwater docking station to the furthest point on the original search field's perimeter, where they erected a decoy base of operations. From there, they strung cables out to an array of lights, boxes, and scientific equipment to give the impression that they were focusing on a point even further away from the abyss.

Falling for this sham, the French team started building a base not far from the Americans' hoax. This tactic duped the next five international teams in the same way.

By the time the American charade was discovered, the *Trieste III* had already located the saucer in its new resting place. To the Americans' delight, their remote units sent back clear images of the alien craft resting comfortably in the middle of a precipice, 21,000 feet beneath the surface.

The American commander, Captain Robert Walsh, continued his smoke and mirror tactics, passing radio traffic with no apparent regard for secrecy. As soon as he was sure of what he had found, the *Trieste III* left the area to hover far downrange from its find, in another attempt to mislead the growing number of international competitors, while his team evaluated the situation.

When the *Trieste III* arrived at its next spurious location, Captain Walsh resumed his bogus communiqués.

"Con, Radio…, we are receiving an emergency action message."

"Radio, Con…, I'm on my way, stand by."

After an appropriate pause, Walsh switched to the 1MC: "Con, this is the captain. Come left to course two-seven-zero. Increase your speed to standard. Make your depth eighteen-fifty, smartly."

"Con…, aye, Captain!"

Detecting this maneuver, the Russian aquanauts promptly jockeyed their tiny DSRV, the *Ipatova*, to see what the Americans were up to. In their haste, the Russians became entangled in one of the umbilical cords that connected several docking stations supporting the panoply of explorers that were scouring about, known as underwater robotic vehicles, or URVs. The ensnarement paralyzed the *Ipatova's* propulsion, causing massive short-circuiting and jeopardizing the Russians' air supply. To their chagrin, they were forced to make a clarion call to the international community for help.

Complications in what should have been just an inconvenient rescue procedure made the incident life-threatening. The Japanese DSRV, the *Chihaya*, succeeded in freeing the entangled Russians with less than one hour of air supply left. Already thoroughly annoyed with the Americans' constant attempts at deceit, the crew of the *Ipatova* would soon discover that this last maneuver was another American charade. This infuriated the Russians, who now blamed the Americans for their near-catastrophe and embarrassment.

The French sub, the *Napoleon*, had been tracking the Americans ever since the *Trieste III* arrived on the scene, plotting and marking every move Walsh made. Shortly after the Americans left their previous location, Captain Jacques Arneau and his crew also located the alien craft.

At first, both teams felt snug with their discovery, the Americans because they thought they had a secret, and the French because they shared the secret unbeknownst to the Americans. Like most secrets on this expedition, it was destined to be short-lived.

As the days in the stormy Atlantic marched into the first month, the exact location of the unobtainable prize became common knowledge. Despite all the high-tech clamoring in the frigid temperatures and extreme pressures 21,000 feet below the surface, the first footholds of any real progress had yet to be made. After seven weeks of failed attempts, numerous equipment collisions, and harsh exchanges among everyone involved, equipment and diplomacy were frayed beyond their already fragile state. The international community did not have the faintest idea what to try next. It had become uncomfortably obvious to everyone that if the feat of raising the craft were to be achieved at all, this could only come about through the collaboration of all the nations, using their combined technologies.

By this time, there were eighteen countries represented by surface craft on the scene. In the previous ten years, there had been several international deep-sea rescue exercises in which most of these same nations had taken part, either as players or observers. Those maneuvers had always been conducted with a spirit of cooperation, but now the unprecedented stakes replaced that congeniality with an attitude of every man for himself. With no other options, however, everyone finally agreed to a meeting. The steel grey sky and chilly winds that whipped the gloomy sea into a mass of contrary whitecaps described the moods of the discordant scientists who gathered that morning aboard the Australian carrier, the *Atlantis*, with Captain Marshall Daringer presiding.

The first few hours of the conference were unproductive, as each country brought its own unacceptable requirements to the table. Eager to dominate the mission, the Russian chief of operations made the first bid to be the project's leader.

"Ladies and gentlemen," he said, "I am Captain Ilya Topolov. One thing we all agree on.... Is our best interest to recover alien craft and unlock secrets. People of Mother Russia absolutely make no objection to share what we find. Fact is, Mother Russia only country in world with tools to oversee operation in such extreme depth. Without mighty *Kursk*, recovery not possible. *Kursk* will allow to monitor all phases of project and provide power to robotics. For this reasons, is clear I should be accepted director of mission."

"We object!" shouted the representative of the UAE in a voice that rose above the clamor of protest that filled the room. "We object to any *one* person or nation being appointed as director!" As the din subsided, the tall, bearded man, wearing a flowing white *dishdasha* with a matching *guthra* on his head, stood up to face the assembly. "We need a board of directors," he insisted, "to ensure that everyone's interests are considered."

"Ridiculous!" countered the British spokesperson, Andrew White-Thomson. "A board of directors will only complicate matters. As for leadership, I personally think my staff would be the best suited for this task. However, a simple drawing of straws to choose a leader will probably be the only way we can get on to the real business at hand."

Again, the grumblings of mixed emotions filled the room.

"Orduh! Orduh, please!" Captain Daringer demanded as he banged his heavy gavel on the podium. "Everyone will get'is turn." As the room settled down, he continued, "We will now 'ear from Mistuh Sumimoto."

"Greetings, fellow scientists," said the short, stout Japanese delegate, bowing to everyone. "My government would also like to be considered for position of director of operations. Without our flotation collar, we will never be able to recover alien craft."

Once again, a rumble of objections erupted from all sides.

Banging his gavel impatiently, Daringer announced, "We are not 'ere to choose a leaduh! The purpose of this meeting is simply to determine 'ow we should proceed to recover the sausuh. Everyone settle down, please. We'll now 'ear from Doctors Cuvier and Lestaire."

Everyone immediately went silent as two stunning French-women rose to speak.

"*Mesdames et messieurs*," began the taller of the two, "*certainement*, vee all concur on zee importance of zis discovery and zat vee must share equally vatever vee find. Mon associate, Doctoresse Michelle Lestaire, and I 'ave a proposal zat veel provide for everyone's concerns in an atmosphere zat veel allow us to..., as our British colleague says..., get to zee real business at hand."

With that, Dr. Lestaire, who spoke perfect English, addressed the audience: "*Bonjour*! Our idea is quite simple. Each nation will have total control over its own part of the project, while contributing its special expertise toward the common goal. The Japanese have a flotation collar that promises to be capable of raising this fantastic craft to the surface. France's contribution will be to connect this collar to the craft, using our deep submergence robots. The Russians will use their bathyscaphe to provide a human overview of the operation as well as a strong command signal to the remote equipment. The British have already begun to construct a mammoth sea dock that will house the alien craft once it has been surfaced. The UAE has generously offered to provide financing for this colossal endeavor, along with many other nations that want to be part of the effort. Of course, we will go along with whatever is decided here, but we believe our plan will allow everyone to feel in control of their interests."

As the eloquent women took their seats, the rapt silence that had fallen over the assembly gave way to a low murmur of assent.

"Well, I must say," observed Daringer from the podium, "that's as good a plan as any I can think of. Are there any objections?"

Amazingly, there was only silence.

Turning to the American delegate, Daringer asked, "Mistuh North, do you 'ave anything to add?"

Without rising from his seat, North replied, "No comment at this time."

Taking advantage of this extraordinary moment, the Aussie captain banged his gavel three times.

"Since there are no objections," he declared, "the French proposal is 'ereby approved as our plan fawr proceeding. Let the work resume timarrow at oh-eight-'undred hours."

While the other countries thought they were attempting to raise an alien craft that was the first real proof of extraterrestrial life, the Americans knew from Dr. Abblett's report that the prize was much more. In fact, it was nothing less than the key to the extraterrestrial origin of Adam and Eve.

From the beginning, Captain Walsh had been following secret orders to keep the saucer out of the reach of the other nations. The *Trieste III* was capable of functioning at 23,000 feet, but aside from coming to rest next to the alien craft, there was little more it could accomplish alone. Walsh's updated orders were to find ways to impede progress until Washington could come up with another solution.

Meanwhile, at the UN and on the surface ships, the Americans were following similar directives, tossing monkey wrenches one after another into the mix whenever possible. In New York, on the floor of the General Assembly, the Americans mounted long diatribes that wore away at the policymakers over insignificant points, such as the patch designs for the unified operation and who would supply the bottled water to the sea dock once it was constructed.

Despite these exasperating tactics, the project was moving forward. After the first of the fifteen-foot flotation collar sections descended to the site, it was carefully placed into position around the massive saucer. Two days would be needed for each of the twenty-one sections to be offloaded on the surface and then placed into position. If everything went without a hitch, the whole operation would take six weeks.

The French and Australian URVs were performing flawlessly, guiding the collar sections into position around the prize. Connecting the sections together would prove more challenging. No one was sure if the robots had the dexterity needed to lock each section to the next, but the Japanese remained confident that the operation, which depended on the design of their flotation collar, could be accomplished.

At this point, the deceptive Americans reported a problem with the *Trieste III*.

"Now hear this," Captain Walsh announced over the common radio band. "We are experiencing a malfunction in our propulsion system. I have decided to go back to Norfolk for repairs. We shall return as soon as possible. That is all."

As the DSRV left the area, the French submarine commander, Captain Arneau, ceased his vigilant tracking of the Americans, certain that he would notice when the *Trieste III* returned.

"And good riddance to you, troublemakers," he mumbled to himself. "Now we can get things done without having to watch your every move."

Soon, hot tempers in the international community were replaced by a spirit of enthusiastic cooperation, especially now that the irritating Americans were no longer on the site.

For the next several days, everything proceeded satisfactorily. Captain Topolov positioned his marvelous bathyscaphe above the prize, affording an excellent overview of the operation. His magnificent instrument illuminated the site with its mighty floodlights while providing a powerful command signal to the URVs as they performed meticulously despite the extreme conditions that exist at 21,000 feet.

The third of the twenty-one collar sections to be delivered was nearly at its destination when the operation had its first serious malfunction. At 19,000 feet, all eight of the URVs inexplicably released their grip, causing the flotation collar section to fall away, missing the precipice altogether and disappearing irretrievably into the abyss.

The whole mission was put on hold while the community scrutinized the mystery of the URVs' failure. Everyone was at a loss to explain the cause of the mishap. However, after a week of fruitless diagnostic checks, the project resumed as before, with the URVs again performing perfectly, staying in close contact with the prize as they delivered each section of the flotation collar 21,000 feet below the surface. Watching from within the bathyscaphe, Captain Topolov and his men were the only people who could actually see—and almost touch—the UFO right outside their portholes.

Two Russian crews alternated, each doing a two-week stint, followed by two weeks of rest and relaxation on the surface. At first, the aquanauts looked forward to these relief periods when they would be flown to Bermuda for their well-deserved time to bask in the sun, surf, and enjoy the female comradeship of the holiday island.

After their third retreat of this kind, however, the Russians found that they were more eager to return to their tight undersea environment than they were to leave it. Ironically, their supposed rest and recuperation only served to agitate them. Distressed by the media's interpretation of their mission, they craved to be back in their undersea tabernacle. The surface world felt to them like an anticlimactic drab reality, compared to the sublime feeling of working on the project to raise the awesome alien craft.

In their frustration, the Russians vented their anger against the Americans. Their memories of those desperate hours entangled in the URV's power line, contemplating their potentially gruesome death before they were rescued in the nick of time, had instilled in them a hunger for revenge.

"If I ever get chance," said one of the crew, "I break their legs and leave them at bottom of sea."

"Yes, we must find way to make American pigs pay for

treachery!" said Vasily Kolchak, the first mate.

But each time the Russians returned to duty in the confines of the bathyscaphe, their simmering rage was quelled by a feeling of well-being and forgiveness, which they were at a loss to explain.

"What going on here?" Topolov wondered. "On surface, we want punish Americans.... Down here we ready to hug them."

Three weeks after the still unsolved URV incident, the placement of the flotation collars was slow but steady. Ten of the twenty-one collar sections lay in place around the saucer, waiting to be connected.

Confirmation that Walsh and his crew had arrived at Norfolk for repairs to the *Trieste III* made everyone in the international mission breathe easier. However, this heartfelt relief was unfounded, for the *Trieste III* had a successor, the *San Francisco*. This state-of-the-art Submarine Rescue Diving Recompression System (SRDRS) was touted for its revolutionary capabilities, which included a silent propulsion technology. Although it had officially been scheduled to be launched in two years, it was, in fact, already in service. Secretly commissioned, she was capable of reaching depths exceeding 30,000 feet. Her top-secret hydro-magneto caterpillar propulsion system, which had no moving parts, was undetectable and extremely fast. Shortly before *The Trieste III* left for Norfolk, Captain Walsh and his crew had covertly met up with the *San Francisco* and transferred aboard.

Everything was going smoothly in the Bermuda Triangle as flotation collar section number 11 started down to its destination. But then, at 19,000 feet, without any indication of a problem, all eight URV units again simultaneously released their grip. Just as before, the collar section fell away, missing the precipice and disappearing into the abyss.

"*Mon Dieu!* Vee 'ave lost zem again!" screamed René Mornault, chief operator of the URVs, into his headset. "Captain Arneau, do you read me? Vee 'ave lost zee collar section. Eet's on eets way to zee bottom!"

Before the French commander could answer, Mr. Sumimoto on the Japanese tender was yelling back into his communicator, "This is unacceptable! How many more sections must we lose? Problem is with French robots. Obviously, they cannot remain constant at these depths."

"Zat is absurd!" retorted Arneau. "Zere is no indication of any such zing. My instruments show a momentary disruption in power. Zuh robots are now operational again.... How can zis be? *Kursk*, vat does your control panel read?"

"*Da*," replied Vladimir Kreshevitz, commander of the second crew of the *Kursk*. "I, too, show momentary disturbance in power signal. Robots operational now. System check show no trouble. No indication what happened. Sonar also show nothing.

I see collar section. It will miss us. Is falling away into abyss."

Captain Topolov and his crew were just arriving on the *Atlantis*, returning from their rest and recuperation in Bermuda. Stunned by the similarity of the mysterious flotation collar mishaps, Topolov, naturally skeptical scientist that he was, could not accept that this seemingly coincidental occurrence was another freak accident. There was something suspicious about this malfunction.

Smells like Walsh, he thought. *But how can be? Walsh hundreds of miles away.*

Topolov's instincts were more accurate than he knew. However, without any clues, it was hard for him to distinguish his intuition from his tendency to blame the tricky Americans for everything.

Once again, Captain Walsh had covertly piloted the silent super-sub to a depth of 24,000 feet, three thousand below the precipice. From this position, using a silent micro-torpedo, he had sabotaged another flotation collar section with a single imperceptible ping. This insidious technology was beyond anything the other countries had. It could not be distinguished from a large fish or any other biologic as it sped along its way.

At this rate, the project could be put off indefinitely while the Americans figured out a way to reach their objective of exclusivity.

Morale was high aboard the *San Francisco*. Listening to the enraged communications now coming from all parties as word of the calamity spread throughout the scientific fleet, Walsh reveled in his success.

"All ahead full!" he ordered.

The *San Francisco* responded with the lithe agility of a great white.

Wanting to try out his magic torpedoes on the URV units when they next appeared over the site, Walsh kept the *San Francisco* close to the sheer sides of the precipice as he maneuvered to his new position, snug in the cloak of silence this new technology afforded him. He had not had so much fun since the beginning of his long career back in the haughty days of the Cold War, when he routinely played deadly games of cat and mouse with his Russian counterparts beneath the polar ice caps. He had cut his teeth during those perilous days, which he always looked back on with a fond nostalgia.

Lost for a moment in those memories, he was jolted back into the present by a sudden crashing vibration amidships. The collision alarm sounded instantly as the boat veered inadvertently to starboard.

"All stop!"

Walsh's order came more as a reflex than a calculated maneuver, but it was too late, since the momentum had already smashed the bantam super-sub into the precipitous walls of the abyss.

The Americans were in big trouble. Walsh had no way of

knowing that it was his own act of sabotage that had come back to bite him. The falling flotation collar section he had shot out of the URV's grasp had slammed into the *San Francisco*. With the impact, an electrical fire immediately broke out in the engine room. As multiple damage reports came into the con, Walsh tried to calculate the possibilities for survival. Anger, bewilderment, urgency, and a dozen other emotions swept through his mind, but panic was not among them.

"We've lost propulsion!" cried the first mate.

"Switch to batteries, all back full!" Walsh commanded.

"Aye, Captain!"

The order was carried out at once, but it was no good. They were wedged in a cleft of the undersea wall, and the limited alternate power source was not enough to break them free. Trapped 27,000 feet below the surface, they were not going anywhere.

Their immediate concern was the toxins that the electrical fire was producing. The crew quickly extinguished the flames, but venting the deadly gasses had left them with less than six hours of air. Walsh almost preferred the inevitable doom they were facing to his only option for rescue.

"Radio, Con! Send out an SOS!"

The recovery teams of all the nations were astonished when they discovered who was sending out the distress signal. Next came the brutal realization that Walsh most likely caused the malfunctions of the URVs. These speculations took up precious moments of the *San Francisco*'s oxygen supply.

Ironically, the only ones with the equipment to make a rescue attempt were the Russians, whom Walsh had nearly killed with his callous antics. In their usual agitated state upon returning from Bermuda, Topolov and his men were not inclined to grasp the urgency of the *San Francisco*'s situation.

"Such shame!" quipped Topolov's first mate. "How project ever succeed now, with Americans lost? Perhaps we send sympathies while they still have radios."

After allowing his men a moment to ventilate, the captain quickly snapped them back into reality.

"We not same as *them*," he said. "And now, there is much to be done! First, we must transfer relief crew from *Kursk* to *Ipatova* to make enough room to rescue scoundrels. This procedure take much time. Despite desire for revenge, we must act quickly to complete mission before is too late. We not same as *them!* Cast off!"

As the Russian rescue sub, the *Ipatova*, began its descent to the *Kursk* at the project site, word was passed among the international fleet that the desperate mission was under way.

"Well," said Captain Daringer on the bridge of the *Atlantis*, "everything that can be done is being done. We'll soon know if those rascals will be lucky enough to survive their predicament, although it would seem that their luck is running out."

Normally under these circumstances, there would be nonstop radio contact with reassurance to the disabled craft that help was on the way. But the only response sent down to the Americans was "Message understood."

This curt reply left no doubt about the lack of compassion

the community felt for the American crew, who had been working so diligently to undermine the whole operation. The obvious absence of any encouragement from the surface sent a jolt of anxiety through Walsh's crew.

At the United Nations, the situation provoked outrage and stinging criticism. More than a few members of the international community pointed out that even this calamity served the Americans' obvious objective of delaying the project. Having been caught red-handed, the Americans could say nothing to curb the disdain being heaped upon them from all sides.

This unfolding story of the roots of mankind, or the "saucer story," as everyone called it, had become the first and longest segment on the daily news programs of every network across the planet—with the exception of the American administration's pet, VoxNet. As the world assimilated each new revelation, an unprecedented fervor and enthusiasm swept over the peoples of the Earth, unifying everyone—including the Americans, who resented having been cast as the villains in this global mission. The wave of negative publicity was of such overwhelming proportions that it caused most of the normally docile American population to demand explanations from the Senate as to why such epithets as *ruthless, inhuman, treacherous,* and *vicious* were being used to describe the character of their country.

Spurred on by popular demand to investigate the matter, the Senate ultimately uncovered Dr. Abblett's report that had been the rationale at the root of the administration's covert maneuvers in trying to retain sovereign control of the project. Once these facts were fully exposed, it became obvious to the conscience-ravaged populace that the policy its government was following was unacceptable.

The people's message was now clear to those Senators who still knew right from wrong. While it was true that Americans had made this extraordinary discovery, the find really belonged to all the peoples of the Earth, and thus America should be a positive contributor to the project, not a saboteur of it.

The spokesmen for the administration argued vehemently for their right as first finders to exclusivity over the project, but each time they repeated their position, its illegitimacy became more evident. The government then presented polls which claimed that the present course of action was the one preferred by most of the country. Nearly every American realized that the truth of the matter was just the opposite. Only a certain marginal segment of the population remained faithful to the government's dictum in spite of all the proof to the contrary. There was no doubt about it: the administration was losing ground with its every move.

The peoples of the Earth were as one, riveted to every new development in the story of this extraordinary discovery. A renaissance was dawning such as the world had never seen before. The rescue attempt unfolding at sea was now the center of this unprecedented international focus.

In the midst of this latest crisis, the Russians noted the familiar feeling of well-being that swept over them whenever they approached the saucer. By the time Topolov was able to transfer the five-man relief crew from the *Kursk* to the *Ipatova*, there was barely time left to locate and rescue the desperate delinquents caught in their own karma at 27,000 feet below.

The *Ipatova* was a unique craft, considerably more maneuverable than the *Kursk,* allowing the aquanauts to use it as a shuttle. This model was also a submarine rescue diving and recompression system (SRDRS), with the capacity to accommodate eight rescuees. However, being limited to depths no greater than 25,000 feet, it would have to wait while the *Kursk* dove the extra two thousand feet to reach the *San Francisco.*

Because the *Kursk* could only accommodate five, retrieving all seven Americans would require Captain Topolov to make two trips back and forth to the *Ipatova*, while the clock ticked out the last of the *San Francisco*'s air supply. This would be a formidable task, whose success would be questionable at best.

As the *Kursk* left the project site without its co-pilot, the *Ipatova*'s powerful floodlights signaled GOOD LUCK GOD-SPEED.

When he reached a depth of 27,000 feet, Topolov began his search by using his powerful twin beams like two flashlights in the pitch blackness to scan the sheer sides of the sea cliff.

Captain Walsh and his crew waited in the frigid depths, anticipating the worst as their air steadily diminished. The silence that had followed the single response to their SOS was unprecedented. While unnerving, the blatant absence of any moral support was not surprising to Walsh, given the subversive role he had played. Remaining steady in the face of impending doom, Walsh now served as the only source of hope to his distressed crew.

When the men finally heard the thick Russian accent instructing them to give a signal for the sonar to home in on, it was as if the voice of God had spoken. With all the sophisticated technologies the super-sub possessed, the only signal they could produce to attract the Russians came from banging a common hammer on the hull—which they did until they heard the *Kursk* connecting to their docking collar. Fortunately, the angle was not severe and the mating was reasonably simple.

It had been thirty-four minutes since the *Kursk* left the *Ipatova* and located the *San Francisco*. Another fifteen minutes passed before the first four Americans squeezed into the tight quarters and the *Kursk* was on her way back to the waiting *Ipatova*. Less than fifty minutes of the *San Francisco*'s air supply remained as Topolov started back down to the troublemaker, this time with the luxury of a co-pilot. After making precise calculations from information given him by the four Americans, Topolov estimated that Walsh and his two men would still have twenty minutes more air supply than what was needed to complete the mission.

Now that the tables had turned, Topolov, confident that he would be able to complete the rescue with minutes to spare, embraced his crew's desire to make the Americans squirm. The Russians would never forget how close they had come to disaster at the hands of those they were about to save. Waiting to open the docking hatch until the estimated cushion of time was cut in half, they would seize the opportunity to give their adversaries a taste of their own medicine. Then, as a final touch, they would scuttle the *San Francisco* by leaving her hatch open. With only minutes to spare, the American spoilers finally heard the sounds of hope as the *Kursk* returned and attached to the *San Francisco*'s docking collar.

After extracting every drop of mental anguish that such close timing could produce, Topolov gathered the demoralized rogues just in time. Captain Walsh and his men could not say enough to express their gratitude, doing all the talking during the ascent to the *Ipatova.* Meanwhile, in silent protest, Topolov and his co-pilot said nothing.

Finally, Walsh took the hint. "I must confess," he said, "that I'm ashamed of the way we Americans have behaved.... All I can say is that I was following orders, and I will no longer do so..., even though it will probably mean the end of my career."

Turning to his co-pilot, Topolov spoke aloud for the first time: "Such career *should* end."

On a summer morning in 1891, the sun rose, illuminating the eastern horizon with its blazing prophecy of another sweltering pass. Aside from startling a multitude of black crows and sending them aloft in all directions, the sudden appearance of the sky barge in the glistening golden meadow went unnoticed. Terran and his away team, disguised in paintball garb, were the first to disembark, carrying the seven-foot triangular time portal down the short ramp to the grassy field. Next came the spindly science officer, Mandoon, looking around like a nervous squirrel, trying to take his surroundings in all at once. So far, the landing zone seemed to be what they had hoped for, secluded and close to the target area.

The space wizard was looking for the ideal spot to set up his time machine. He chose one about twenty-five yards from the bend of the Napa River near a patch of ferns—the same area they had selected on their preliminary scans from space. As far as they could tell, this spot would still be relatively untouched when they arrived one hundred and sixteen years in the future. However, they would not know for certain until they activated the time portal.

Meanwhile, as Terran and Zalcon came down the ramp, they were going over their list of priorities. On the one hand, time was a factor they could adjust as needed to accomplish all they had come to do. On the other hand, their digestive systems gave them little more than seventy-two hours to complete the mission before the Smart Pills lost their effect.

Terran and Zalcon watched and waited for their science officer to work his magic on the stolen piece of Illuminosity technology.

"Mandoon's confidence has been improving steadily," said Zalcon, "ever since that fiasco with Rosario."

"Yes," Terran said, nodding, "he really is a very efficient study. Let bygones be forgotten."

After setting his beacons in a tight fifteen-foot circumference around the magic triangle, Mandoon announced to his captain, "Everything is ready to go, sir."

Terran responded immediately: "Transport team, remain here to guard the ship and wait for our return. Away team, take your positions." As soon as all six of the away team were ready, Terran shouted to Mandoon, "Let's go!"

There was an immediate crack of blinding white light.

They were still standing twenty-five yards from the river-bank, but the scene had changed. The sky barge was gone, and the golden meadow was now cultivated farmland, mostly cov-ered with vineyards and connected by a dirt road that had not been there before. A lofty stand of pines, where the patch of ferns had been, served to conceal the time portal from all angles except from the river.

The next objective of the mission was to locate and recon-noiter the Paintball Jungle, which, according to their calcula-tions, was no more than a mile upriver.

Terran left Mandoon and one crew member to guard the time portal. "Stay alert and out of sight," he instructed. "If anyone or anything should come by, you know what to do. We won't be long."

Posting themselves strategically behind the pines, Mandoon and his mate watched and waited. Their orders were simple. Ter-ran's indirect command meant only one thing: instant extermi-nation.

This first recon was to get the big picture of the facility. Next, Zalcon would go in alone, posing as a paintball player. He would have to confirm the presence of the three men they had come for, then figure out how to abduct them. Following the riverbank northward, they soon came upon a lush stand of eucalyptus trees, the grove extending as far upriver as they could see.

Excited that his expectations were unfolding without a hitch, Terran said, "This must be it! I recognize these trees from the website."

The exotic environment invigorated the away team. The majestic trees along the Napa River were a refreshing contrast to their latest stint in space. With the river now at their backs, they penetrated the awesome maze of paintball fortifications scattered throughout the golden green forest.

Passing the first large fort, Zalcon confirmed their progress according to the field map that he had obtained from the Jungle's website, which indicated every aspect of the facility.

"That must be what they call Fort Davey Crockett," he said. "According to this, we are heading for the staging area."

A short march brought them past the other indicated landmarks until they came to the twelve-foot screens that marked the front of the playing field. Next came the main road, which separated the playing field from the parking area. The obvious structure in the middle of the extensive staging area was the supply shack. It was there that they anticipated finding the ones they had come for. But since it was still early in the morning, there was no one about except for a lone white vehicle wending its way toward them, leaving a dust cloud in its wake.

As the SUV went by, the occupants were unaware that they were being watched from behind the green protective screens.

"We'll need such a vehicle to fit in here and complete the disguise," Terran said. "Let's go!"

As the away team filed out through the narrow opening in the screens, the early arrivals already had their gear spread out on the tailgate.

"Good morning," Zalcon said, catching them by surprise with his mundane greeting.

Startled by the Maraudians' sudden appearance when they approached on foot with no visible means of transportation, the two players answered with a hint of suspicion: "Good morning."

Without missing a beat, Zalcon asked, "When does this place open for business?"

Although his question sounded reasonable to the players, it did not quell their intuitive apprehension.

"Not for another hour or so. We like to come early and get all set up. Are you guys here to play?"

Terran nodded as Zalcon continued, "We're here to look the place over. We want to see how it works."

The two sportsmen glanced at each other when they heard this sketchy response. The one closer to Terran asked, "How did you guys get here?"

Ignoring their question, Terran nodded to Zane.

The men never knew what hit them as Zane immediately drew his handgun and stunned the pair, dropping them where they stood. Quickly collecting the Earthlings' equipment, the away team tossed it into the rear of the vehicle.

"Right!" Zane said. "Pick them up and let's get back to the

river."

Following orders, the burly six-foot-two Maraudians effortlessly threw the unconscious sportsmen over their shoulders, as everyone but Zalcon retreated back through the jungle the way they had come. Zalcon jumped into the driver's seat and, after a moment's recollection, started the vehicle and jerked it into gear. Following his nose, the first officer had no trouble finding his way out to the main road and toward the river. Presently, Terran and the away team came along, carrying the prisoners, who were still unconscious.

After a short consultation to reconfirm the next phase of the operation, Terran and his men continued back toward the bend in the river. Checking his credit card and matching driver's license, Zalcon drove to the park to figure out the remaining unknowns while posing as a paintball player.

The staging area was steadily filling up with cars and enthusiastic players when he parked the white SUV directly in front of the supply shack. He seemed as regular as any of the others standing in line, waiting to pay admission. But among the many paintballers this day, he was the only one who had come for something other than fun and therapy.

According to the information on his liability waiver, he was Michael Kelly, a reporter for the *San Francisco Chronicle*. After renting a top-of-the-line equipment package, he attended the mandatory orientation, tied a red band on his arm, and followed some fifty other red teammates out to their flag station to play the first game of the day.

As is often the case for the typical first-timer, "Kelly" was eliminated early in the game. Noticing his confusion about what to do next, Andrew, the referee, directed him off the playing field.

"Just head back to the staging area," Andrew said, "and get cleaned up for the next game."

Nodding, Zalcon asked him a typical question: "Does Magic Carpet Bob play in these games?"

"Sometimes," Andrew answered, "Bob plays in the flag games, but he always plays in the Beeswax game, after lunch."

"Kelly" followed with another often-asked question: "What's the Beeswax game?"

After he was informed about the traditional first game after lunch, his next question was not so typical, and Andrew, always a keen observer of human nature, took notice.

"What about Magic Carpet Bob's sons?" asked the imposter. "Do they ever all play together?"

Without revealing his suspicion, Andrew briefly explained that the Beeswax was the one game that all three always played together. But when he returned to the shack after the game, he took Zoe aside and told him about the curious stranger.

Zoe's eyebrows went up. "Which one is he?" he asked. "Point him out."

Andrew directed Zoe's gaze to the front counter, where Zalcon was poring over the brochures.

"What's with *this* guy?" Zoe asked Eli, who was working at the fill station in the rear of the shack.

"Why, what's up?" Eli asked as Zoe nodded toward the man.

"He's asking questions about *us*. Wants to know if you and I ever play with Dad in the game."

Eli's eyebrows also rose with the wary sense that always accompanied unwanted inquiries. Bob and his sons were especially touchy about strangers asking questions about them since their visit from the Feds. They were now reluctant to make new acquaintances, which was contrary to their usual outgoing nature.

As Eli picked up the microphone to announce the assignments for the second game of the day, Zoe put on an orange referee's vest, telling his brother, "I'll check this dude out."

"Kelly" joined his teammates once again as they headed out to their next starting point, with Zoe following the inquisitive one from a distance. Right from the start of the game, Zoe was impressed with the stranger's savvy as he "ran the ribbon," a move that always yielded good results because it entailed circumnavigating the borders of the playing field. Requiring speed and distance for success, the maneuver was one that most players avoided. Also, such a move did not allow for the more instant gratification of rushing up the center to a quick engagement with the opposing team.

At first, Zoe wondered if this player knew what he was doing from experience. "Kelly" was moving with an agility that would ensure every advantage a maneuver like this had to offer. Zoe caught up with him in time to see him enter the opposition's unguarded flag station and snatch the object of everyone's focus.

As soon as he grabbed the gold silken swatch, "Kelly" proceeded down the center of the playing field, slowing somewhat to the pace that stealth required for survival. Zoe was impressed with the level of skill this newcomer was revealing as "Kelly" made his way toward the concentrated firefight ahead.

With golden rays of sunlight shooting through the lavish canopy to the jungle floor, the stranger's moves were like those of a cat as he avoided the light and slipped through the shadows. Taking advantage of the cover provided by the teepees and bunkers that had been arranged from the fallen eucalyptus trees, he was able to close in undetected. Not only did he have possession of the opposition's flag, he was also about to come up on the green team from behind, a rare advantage that was always considered most desirable by any experienced paintballer.

Not wanting to spoil such a skillfully earned position, Zoe kept far enough behind to ensure that he would not give "Kelly" away as the stranger came upon his first three victims, obliging them to surrender without firing a shot.

Following a little closer, Zoe realized that he had never seen such skillful plays being executed one after another. After "Kelly" had come up behind each of the first green players and stuck his gun in their back, he had told them to surrender just loud enough that no one but his mark had heard him. Thankful of being spared the extra sting of being shot up close, they had all complied immediately.

By now, the imposter's own base was in clear view. Although the green team had already lost half its numbers, it would soon be in possession of the red team's flag. There were only six red defenders left, fighting desperately to prevent the inevitable, when "Kelly" unleashed his fire, dealing two paintballs in lightning succession to each green player with all the precision of a pro. So fast was his delivery that the end was at hand before anyone realized what had happened.

Zoe was flabbergasted. He had seen and performed many amazing tactics in his nineteen-year career, but this was a day of days. Even so, when it was over, he returned to the shack without acknowledging his amazement or otherwise letting his presence be known to this mysterious paintball warrior.

Eli could see from the expression on his brother's face that something extraordinary had occurred.

"Well," he asked, "what happened?"

In all, five flag games were played before it was time to break for lunch. Greatly impressed with Zoe's report of the new-comer's skills, Eli would have followed "Kelly" around to see his style for himself, but the understated athlete never went back out to play. Instead, after scutinizing everything the pro shop had to offer, he asked for a green observer's vest.

"Aren't you going to play the next game?" Zoe asked.

"I plan on playing in the big game after lunch," he said. "Until then, I want to gather material for an article I'm writing about paintball."

Passing him the observer's vest, Zoe asked, "What other fields have you played at?"

"I'm new at this. It's my first time."

Again, Zoe's eyebrows rose with consternation, but not wanting to reveal his suspicions, he let the answer go unchallenged.

As "Kelly" walked off, studying a field map, Zoe turned to his brother. "Man," he said, "this dude is a piece of work."

"Yeah," said Eli, "from what you've told me, he has all the earmarks of a pro. I wonder what his angle is."

"Gathering material for an article sounds plausible," Zoe said, "but the moves he was making out there were just too slick for any first-time player. There's something fishy about this guy."

The long sonorous call of the conch announced the beginning of the afternoon session.

"Get your guns, get your gear, the big game of the day is here!"

This was the fourteen hundredth and twenty-third time that the traditional summons to the Beeswax sounded over the P.A. speakers at the Paintball Jungle.

It was another banner day in the lush eucalyptus grove. Responding to the call to action were some two hundred paintballers, all gathering in front of the target range. This time, there were thirty Hornets standing behind Magic Carpet Bob as he explained the scenario to the first-timers, who made up a third of the anxious Hornet hunters. The Beeswax was always the first game after lunch. The half-hour scenario was a nineteen-year tradition and a paintball phenomenon that featured the renowned San Francisco Hornets, of whom Magic Carpet Bob was the captain.

"The Hornets," Bob announced, "are the largest paintball team in the world, with over four thousand members. Anyone can apply for membership, but it takes three months to get accepted. During that time, we watch applicants, not for their ability with a paintball gun, but for their performance in three distinct areas of our great combat sport. We watch to see how they handle themselves, how they treat their opponents, and how they react when it's their turn to bite the bullet. If they can perform positively in these three areas, bringing fun and a little class to the game, they will have no trouble finding their way into the Great Hive."

This part of the orientation never failed to produce a few new applicants. The Beeswax was a single-flag scenario. The Hornet hunters started with possession of the flag at their base. Their objective was to still possess the flag at the end of the game. To win, the Hornets needed to capture the flag and hang it back at their own base.

"It's not important who wins," Bob said. "What *is* important is that we all have fun and feel good about the way we treat each other out there. So, what do you say we try for our best game *yet*? What do you say?"

"Yeah!" they shouted.

"What do you say?" Bob repeated, pumping them up.

"YEAH!"

"Are you ready?"

"*YEAH!*"

"Alright, let me ask the Hornets if *they're* ready." Turning to his thirty black-and-gold uniformed Bees, he set the psychological hook by asking them, "Hornets, are *you* ready?"

They all responded like a Russian drill team, "YEAH!"

"How fast is fast?"

The unified response came like a clap of thunder: "FAST!"

"San Francisco…"

"HORNETS!"

The team's crisp, energetic response never failed to fill the horde of Hornet hunters with angst, which, together with the Hornets' clever battle tactics, usually enabled the vastly outnumbered swarm to be victorious.

While everything appeared routine as the two teams dispersed to their starting positions, the three top Hornets were preoccupied. The Jungle had always been their sanctuary from the world and its absurdities. Now they were caught in a snarl of futility, feeling an increasing state of anxiety that could no longer be quelled by their passion for the game.

As the world was becoming more and more enthralled with the remarkable events unfolding out at sea, Bob and the boys were becoming increasingly resentful about being excluded from their discovery. At first, the threat of federal imprisonment made them more than willing to detach from their unprecedented find, but as the current events were reported in the top news story every night, they found it impossible to remain indifferent.

The international project that they had brought to the world's attention, which was now their forbidden fruit, had worked its way back into the foreground of their daily thoughts.

"Who would have guessed," Zoe said, "when we snapped those pictures, that we would be forbidden to even talk about this? What a deal!"

Zoe was the bitterest of the three about their situation, but it was eating away at his dad and brother as well. Lately, no matter what they did, their frustration tainted everything. Even now, when the game had been in full swing for twenty of its thirty minutes, and paintballs were flying everywhere like enraged yellow jackets, stinging everyone they could find, the forbidden subject surfaced.

During the intense firefight as the trio provided cover for their team's assault on the Hornet hunters' base, Zoe's mind was elsewhere. He kept up his barrage until all of his one hundred and fifty rounds were expended. Flipping the lid open on his empty hopper, he let his teammates know.

"Loading!"

His focus and movements were mechanical as he drew another pod full of paintballs from his ammo belt.

"There must be some way to reclaim our rightful place in all of this!" he said aloud. Zoe had never been so preoccupied that he had to talk about it even while in the throes of the flag grab.

"Loading!" Eli announced, popping open the top of his pod and pouring the paintballs into his hopper. "Forget about it, Zoe. You heard the man. If we try to bring out our story, our only *rightful place* will be Leavenworth."

"*Tequila!*"

Bob was passing the Hornet code word, which meant they had possession of the flag, and it was time to return to the base and hang it.

"Eli's right," Bob said. "There's nothing we can do. Let's go!"

The center squad had punched through under heavy fire and snatched the flag. As the Bees tried to return the way they had come, the Hornet hunters still had sufficient numbers to thwart their attempt. The Hornets were in a footrace back to their flag station.

In the Beeswax, Bob and his sons always played with the squad on the right, known as the *Sanchos*, or the ones who come in the back door. Their moves had become second nature, which was obvious by the way they covered each other while they fought their way back.

As usual, Bob drew the opponents' fire first, staying behind almost too long to survive. Then, at the crucial moment, he broke and ran from his pursuers, leading them into close quarters with Zoe and Eli, who remained concealed until they were so close that the hunters were stunned to see the Hornet brothers rise in their midst, raking the field with a torrent of paintballs, leaving nowhere to escape the colorful *tsunami*. Unrelenting, they repeated this maneuver all the way back to the fort, greatly decreasing the opponents' numbers in the bargain.

With only minutes left, the game was far from over. As was

often the case, the opposing team managed to have a squad waiting for the flag party, stopping the flag runner at the gates of vic-
tory. But Bob and his boys had a special move for this scenario.

"*El Sancho!*" Bob called.

The Hornet codeword was the directive for the three to make
a wide sweep, avoiding the base altogether, working their way
around to the rear gate, where they would wait for the flag party
to attack the front.

The flag party was two minutes behind as the *Sanchos* waited
in position. Despite their preoccupation, the Hornet commanders were performing another tactic that, after nineteen years,
they could execute routinely. From behind their concealment of
thick underbrush, Zoe continued to stew.

"They'll have the saucer surfaced any day now," he said. "I
wonder if we'll be allowed to see it then."

Topping off his hopper, Eli answered his agitated brother:
"They told us that when the time was right, they would acknowl-
edge us. What else can we do?"

"Alright," Bob said. "Enough! Get ready to rock."

He was referring to what would be the last firefight of the
game. As the flag party arrived back at their base, they realized
it was not over yet. Suddenly, the air was thick with hundreds of
paintballs seeking their targets.

Looking at Zoe, Bob said, "Remember, it's not over till it's
over! Let's go!"

Inside the Hornet base, there were a dozen opponents focusing on the flag party, which consisted of six Hornets, the sole

survivors of the left and center squads. As the firefight intensi-
fied, it became obvious that the right squad was absent. This
could only mean one of two things: either they had been wiped
out, or they were in position.

Brett, the left squad leader, called to his fighters, "*El Sueño!*"

His call, "The Dream," was code for telling them to keep the
attention of their opponents, in the hope that the *Sanchos* were
in position.

"*El Sueño!*" Brett called once again as they laid a veritable
wall of paint into the front of the fort.

This last-ditch effort kept their opponents suspended for a
split second—just long enough for the *Sanchos* to creep up to
the rear gate and catch them by surprise.

"Howdy, boys!"

As Magic Carpet Bob hollered his signature battle cry, the
Sancho trio let loose, double tapping their hair triggers, spray-
ing their opponents with a torrent of twenty-one paintballs per
second that left no survivors. A moment before the horn blared
game's end, the Hornet flag runner entered the fort and hung the
flag.

This was usually a jubilant moment for all the surviving
Hornets, but today Bob and the boys were still brooding over
their unresolved conversation. As they walked off the field, they
were oblivious to the lone Hornet hunter who had been following behind them all this time, watching but never making the
move that would have made all the difference in the outcome of
the game.

The next time they saw "Kelly," the day still had a few hours of play left, but he was already turning in his rental gear.

Zoe stepped up to handle the transaction. "Leaving early?" he asked.

"Yes, but I'll be back tomorrow with my friends. I just wanted to see the layout and get a little practice, so I can have an edge on them."

"How did you like the Beeswax game?"

Without hesitation, "Kelly" said, "It was great, but I didn't last long. Maybe I'll do better tomorrow."

Satisfied with this answer, Zoe handed over the receipt. "Yeah," he said, "well, if you're not dying, you're not trying."

With a smile, Kelly said, "Right. I'll see you tomorrow."

With that he got into the white SUV, gave a friendly wave, and was off.

Now that all of the fifteen-foot sections of the flotation collar had been successfully delivered and placed in position around the prize, there was a new problem facing the international task force. An irreparable glitch caused by the frigid waters and extreme pressure present at 21,000 feet impeded the URVs' ability to manipulate the latching mechanisms.

Although no one was to blame this time for the unforeseeable equipment failure, tempers started to flare now that the project was once again at a standstill. But an astonishing turn of events quelled all frustration when, to everyone's amazement and delight, the disdained Americans redeemed themselves by unveiling a pair of top-secret atmospheric diving suits. Capable of lowering a human operator to a depth of 22,000 feet, the suits also had the dexterity needed to connect the flotation collar sections. This new American technology, together with the Russian bathyscaphe, could accomplish the mission. This contribution considerably restored the Americans' reputation in world opinion.

The new suits allowed the divers to perform with such agility that the first two sections were connected in less than two days.

On the surface, so long as the water remained calm, the construction of the sea dock was also making steady progress. But when weather conditions became adverse, sometimes for days, progress ground to a halt. As the weeks wore on, it was anyone's guess which project would be finished first.

As Terran and Zane watched the white SUV approaching on the dirt road to the stand of pines by the river, their two prisoners were beginning to come around.

Noticing their movement, Terran nodded to Zane. "Hit them again," he ordered.

The lieutenant responded without a word, raising his weapon and stunning the pair with another short blast. The away team, except for Mandoon, gathered around the vehicle as Zalcon got out and made his report.

"We have what we need, Captain. I know the place and time to catch the trio together and away from everyone else. We can enter from the north road and come up behind them."

Terran smiled. "Well done, Commander. We'll leave immediately. Give the coordinates to Mandoon."

The time portal made it possible to treat reality like a movie that the Maraudians could rerun at will. The space wizard made the necessary adjustments to his marvelous machine to return the away team to the previous hour. Soon they were in position behind the Hornet base, where Zalcon had hidden the first time, waiting for the trio to appear as the moment of opportunity repeated itself.

"Here they come!" Zalcon whispered. "Everybody down!"

Bob and the boys came slashing through the underbrush as the Maraudians ducked out of sight behind a woodpile.

Once again, the three Hornets took up their positions behind their flag station and waited with their backs to the aliens. Zalcon boldly stepped out into plain view, purposely snapping a twig beneath his feet for attention.

Zoe, who was the first to see the Hornet hunter, reacted accordingly. "Behind us!" he shouted.

As the other two swung around and leveled their weapons, Zoe recognized the intruder. "Kelly!"

As "Kelly" approached, he appeared to be weaponless. But even more shocking, he was not wearing the mandatory goggles. This most serious violation of the safety rules kept the trio from unleashing their barrage. At the same moment, Zalcon fired his sonic blaster, stunning his hapless victims unconscious.

As the away team returned to the bend in the river, carrying their latest catch, the first two abductees were beginning to stir once again.

Terran was intent as his men regrouped around the time portal. There was still much to be done before they could achieve their ultimate goal.

"Alright," he said, "we've got what we came for.... Let's get back to the ship."

Waiting at the controls of the time portal, Mandoon replied, "Everything is ready, Captain."

"What about *them*?" Zalcon asked, pointing to the two paintball players lying on the ground near their SUV.

Terran never gave them a second glance. "Leave them! Let's go!"

Once again, the away team stood in a tight grouping around the magic triangle, carrying their comatose prisoners like potato sacks over their shoulders.

Pausing for a moment to review the specific requirements of time portal reentry, Mandoon said, "We should hold the Earthlings standing up, so we can remember their position in case we need them when we return for the crystals."

Terran smiled. "Very well. Make it so."

Zalcon gave the two on the ground a last look. "*They'll* have a few questions when they come around," he said with a chuckle.

"That's *their* problem," Terran said as he turned to Mandoon.

"Let's be on our way!"

Mandoon cackled maniacally. "Here we go!"

The instantaneous crack of white light vanished as they appeared in front of the sky barge, startling their two guards.

"That didn't take long!" one said.

Still cackling, Mandoon explained, "Going into the future has a shorter duration, just as the opposite is true. It's the trapezoidal effect."

As the team scurried aboard with their captives, the saucer took off, leaving the golden meadow to resume its tranquility.

Bob and the boys awoke experiencing tingling pins and needles in the midst of unfamiliar surroundings. All they could tell was that they were in a tight compartment of some kind.

"What's happening?" Bob asked, groggy but coherent.

"Where are we?" Zoe muttered. "Kelly! It was that dude from the *Chronicle*!"

As if on cue, the compartment hatch rolled to one side, and "Kelly" stepped in. No longer in camouflage, his cerulean and crimson garb bespoke the flare of a swashbuckler.

"Gentlemen," he announced to the three men on the floor, "allow me to introduce myself. I am Commander Zalcon of the starship *Maraudor*, and you are my prisoners."

Three jaws dropped as the Earthlings sat frozen in wide-eyed amazement. Zoe was the first to respond, looking at Eli with consternation. "I *told* you there was something about this guy," he said.

Eli answered with a glare as Zalcon continued, "You are here because it seems that you possess certain information that we require. Without further delay, I would like you to follow me to the captain and divulge all you can about what we want to know."

Still disoriented, they could hardly believe what was happening to them. The shock of this fantastic moment was masked by Zalcon's congenial tone and matter-of-fact explanation of his intentions.

"This way, please, gentlemen," Zalcon directed.

The trio followed the commander down the passageway, while two crew members who were waiting outside the compartment brought up the rear. To say that Bob and his sons were spooked would have been a gross understatement. As they walked in silence down the strange blue-lit corridor, they took in their surroundings with awed apprehension. When they arrived on the bridge, all three were overwhelmed by the view of the blue and white sphere, which they immediately realized was Earth.

"We're in space!" Zoe gasped.

"My God!" Bob said. "Look at the moon!"

"Unbelievable!" said Eli.

Terran was eager to proceed, but granted them a few moments before breaking their spellbound amazement.

"It has come to our attention," he finally said, "that you have located a Lamorian time ship. What we require from you is its exact location and any other information about it that you may have."

"He must be talking about the saucer," Bob said, looking at Zoe and Eli.

Nodding, Eli said, "The time ship, as you call it, is not where we originally discovered it. An earthquake has shifted its location, and it is presently the focal point of an extensive deep-sea recovery effort."

Knowing that it would have been impossible to retrieve the time ship himself, since he had no technology for operating underwater, Terran was elated by this news. "Where is it now?" he asked.

"We don't know for sure," said Bob, "but we believe it slipped into the abyss."

"How soon will they recover it?"

"We have no way of knowing that," said Zoe.

"We only know what they say on the news," Eli added.

Satisfied that the Earthlings were giving him their full cooperation, Terran made an effort not to appear intimidating. "I imagine you are curious," he said, "how we learned about your secret discovery…and how we found *you*."

The three of them just looked puzzled.

"Does the name Rosario mean anything to you?"

Bob responded, "We've heard the name. Under hypnosis, we learned that he was someone we met while we were marooned on an island somewhere. But we don't actually remember him."

At this point, Zane brought in two men who were dressed like nineteenth-century pirates.

"Captain Rosario and Mister Knox," Terran asked, "do you know these men?"

Looking perplexed, the two pirates shook their heads.

"We never seen 'em before, Cap'n," Knox said.

"And you three…, do you know *these* two?"

Dad and the boys shook their heads.

"Very well, that will be all, Zane."

"Yes, Captain," said Zane, who left the bridge, with Rosario and Knox following behind.

"I have many questions for you, gentlemen," Terran said, "and you may know the answers to some of them without realizing it."

"Are you going to hypnotize us?" Dad asked apprehensively.

Terran could see that the only way to get the big picture from these three would be to subject them to the mind-scanning device known as the Hat. Knowing that their anxiety would only make the sessions more difficult, he assumed a conciliatory tone.

"Although your presence here," he said, "is not of your own choosing, I assure you, I will set you free when we complete this mission."

These comforting words had the desired effect as the trio clung to the hope of Terran's promise.

"But enough for now," the space pirate concluded. "You may return to your quarters for food and rest. We will continue our business after you are refreshed."

The three captives obediently followed Zalcon back to their quarters.

As the hatch to the compartment rolled shut, Zoe said, "So, let me get this straight. We're on a starship orbiting Earth. We're prisoners of these humans from space, who speak English as well as we do, and they're somehow mixed up with the saucer and those two pirates, Rosario and Knox. And now we're gonna give answers to questions we don't know anything about."

"That about sums it up," said Bob.

The absurdity of Zoe's accurate statement was riveting.

"One thing is certain," Eli added. "We'll be reported missing back home. I'm sure the media will be interested in what we have to say now…, *if* we ever make it back."

"Seeing Rosario and Knox didn't ring any bells," Bob mused, holding his head in his hands, trying to make sense of it all. "They didn't recognize us, either. How is it that the captain knows both of our stories? Lots of questions, no answers, and here we are, out in space. I can't *imagine* what's gonna happen next."

Once again, as if on cue, the hatch opened and two crew members entered, carrying trays of food and drink. Without saying a word, they set these down and withdrew.

Zoe was first to sniff the food and the beverage. To his surprise, the aromas were quite agreeable, though unrecognizable.

As the *Maraudor* continued its silent orbit of the Earth in the year 1819, the bridge was buzzing with speculations and anticipations about how to proceed with the mission. Surrounded by

Zalcon, Mandoon, and Zane, Terran tried to prioritize the list of questions they would put to the Earthlings.

"First," he said, "we will get *their* version of what happened on that island."

"Yes, Captain," Zane said, "and we will need to know what the plans are on the surface when the time ship is recovered. I don't think any of the earthmen are aware of its precious cargo. If that *is* the case, we should continue to keep these three in the dark about it."

Zane's point was well taken.

"I suggest," Mandoon said, "that we proceed immediately with the mind scans. The pertinent questions will become evident as they reveal their story. Of course, we will let them sleep first, and then we will start with the father."

Meanwhile, the trio was debating whether or not to trust the food.

"Man, I'm hungry!" Zoe said. "But how do we know they didn't put something in this stuff?"

"I was thinking the same thing," said Eli.

"If they were gonna do away with us," Bob said, "I think they would have done it by now. They want information from us, so they certainly wouldn't kill us."

"Not yet, anyway," said Zoe. "Let's eat!"

"Okay. So, who's gonna go first?" asked Eli.

"I'll go first," said Bob.

"No, we all go together, or not at all," Zoe said. "And I'm much too hungry for not at all."

Stifling their paranoia, they proceeded to devour all of the alien cuisine.

Then they drifted into a dreamless sleep in the bunks of their claustrophobic compartment.

They were abruptly wakened with no idea how long they had slept when the hatch rolled open and Zalcon entered.

"We require you to undergo some passive questioning," he explained. "It is a process that will allow us to know everything you have experienced, even though you may not be aware of it yourselves. But I assure you, there's nothing to fear. You'll find the process painless and easy."

Zalcon's explanation did not make them feel any the less fearful, but their overall condition of helplessness gave them no alternative.

"You will be first," he said, pointing to Bob.

"No worries," Bob said. "I don't know anything, so this shouldn't take long."

As Zalcon left with Bob, Zoe and Eli remained sitting sullenly on their bunks.

Following the commander to the science deck, Bob got his first extensive look at the interior of the vessel. As the two made their way through the maze of passages and workstations, the soft sounds and warbles of the ship's technology, along with its cool blue lighting, gave Bob the impression of being in a submarine. A circular elevator without walls, which resembled a giant old-fashioned phonograph player with a central post, lifted them three decks. As they ascended, Bob was afforded glimpses of parts of the ship whose functions he could not even begin to imagine. A short walk brought them to the three-tiered science deck, by far the largest section of the ship he had seen, except for the hangar deck.

Mandoon and Terran were waiting with several technicians next to some exotic equipment, which included several video screens, a large transparent sphere four feet in diameter, control panels, and a Roman-style dining couch covered in a plush fabric resembling fur. As in the rest of the ship, the cool blue lighting gave the whole environment a cold and sterile feeling.

As Bob and Zalcon entered, Terran smiled.

The spindly space wizard was astonished. *A smile on the captain's face,* he thought, *is as rare as the Esseen Crystals themselves.*

Bob noticed for the first time that the captain's tall bearded image resembled that of a Persian prince.

"I trust," said Terran, "that Commander Zalcon has explained why you are here. Holding up what looked like the headpiece of a medieval executioner, he continued, "This is a mind-scanning device we call the Hat. This amazing tool will divulge everything you have experienced in your life as it scrolls through your brain with a painless ease that you will hardly notice. All that is required of you is to recline on the couch and remain open to dwelling upon whatever thoughts we may suggest to you..., nothing more."

"Simple enough," Bob said, trying to sound casual, although that was far from what he was feeling. "I must say, you have some amazing technology."

Bob donned the fantastic headgear and sat back on the Roman-style couch. Wearing the Hat was effortless, with only the dull sensation of many nodes making contact with his head.

The information that Terran was looking for was not easy to locate within the sea of Bob's subconscious memories. It took nearly all of the first session with the Hat before Terran finally reached the area that concerned him. In the final quarter of the two-hour session, images of an island, and then of Rosario and his crew, began to appear.

"Captain," said Mandoon excitedly, "this corroborates what we have already extracted from Rosario and Knox."

"I agree," said Terran. "But enough for now. Take him back to his quarters and let him rest while we take a closer look at this data."

As Bob was escorted from the science deck by two of the technicians, the Maraudian officers sensed that their moment to possess the most sought-after prize in the Universe was at hand.

"I never dreamed," said Terran, his blood racing, "that we would ever come this close to possessing the fabulous crystals! On second thought, we *won't* wait for him to complete another sleep cycle."

"Agreed, Captain," said Mandoon. "But we must not jeopardize his mental stability until we have what we need from him to ensure our success."

"Yes, Captain," Zane said. "We must let him rest a while before going any further."

"Very well," Terran conceded, "a couple of hours, then.... No more."

Bob's next mind scan was even more productive. Huddled around the sphere, the Maraudians talked in hushed tones as they watched the trio find the submerged time ship and then become marooned on a Jurassic island. When they viewed Bob and the boys' rediscovery of the Lamorian vessel at the base of the volcano, they were ecstatic.

"There it is!" whispered Zalcon. "No doubt about it..., they found the saucer, and the crystals *have* to be inside!"

"Yes, Commander," said Terran, "we are on the verge of something great. Please continue."

"Sons of Qwarz!" shouted Zalcon. "He's being torn to shreds by saber-toothed cats! They're eating him alive! How can this be? How can he still be here among us?"

"Quiet!" snapped Terran. "You'll disturb the subject."

The Maraudians were at a loss to understand what they were seeing as the sphere suddenly went transparent.

"Of course!" said Mandoon. "This is the result of the time spike. Remember, Captain, when we saw the first time spike? The second one appeared before the first in the time line. That could only mean that these men returned unscathed to a new variation of their reality with no recollection of what had happened to them."

"Yes, Commander," Terran responded, "that would explain it."

Suddenly, the sphere came alive as the story seemed to be

unfolding once again from the beginning.

"What's happening? asked Zane. "We've already seen their underwater discovery of the saucer. Why is it starting over again?"

"No..., look!" said Zalcon. "It's *not* the same. This time, they're returning safely to harbor."

Gazing into the sphere, they watched the rest of Bob's story up until the present, including his hypnosis sessions with the family doctor and his encounter with the government agents regarding the now classified information.

"That's all he can give us," Terran said. "Zalcon, take him back and bring in the older son for his session."

When Bob arrived at his quarters, he was tired but otherwise unaffected by the examination.

"You're next," Zalcon said, pointing at Eli. "Come with me."

Eli stood up and shot an anxious look at his father.

"No worries, son," Bob said. "It's like I told you. They'll just ask you a few questions. It's harmless."

When Zalcon and Eli arrived on the science deck, it was obvious to the first officer by the look in Terran's and Mandoon's eyes that they were in the throes of the Rapture, focused from within by a raging intoxication. However, Eli noticed nothing of this because, on the surface, the Maraudians seemed calm.

With a friendly smile, Terran said to Eli, "This won't take long. All we want from you is a little information. Then you and your family will be free to go. Sit here, please."

When Eli sat back on the couch, Mandoon placed the Hat on

his head.

"Think back," said Terran, "to your visits to Doctor Abblett."

As Eli pictured himself lying down in the doctor's office, preparing to be hypnotized, the Maraudians started the scan. They began by scrolling from that point back to Eli and Zoe's encounter with the Lamorians. As the story unfolded of their own mythology, which reaffirmed the existence of the cradle race and the fabulous Esseen Crystals, the Maraudians were euphoric.

When it was Zoe's turn to wear the Hat, the Maraudians focused on what had taken place between him and the Lamorians. The ancient people were clearly pleased by the fact that Zoe and his brother came from a time so far ahead in the Lamorians' future—clear proof that their attempt to propagate the human race on Earth had succeeded.

The space pirates then witnessed a ceremony in which the Lamorians took locks of hair and recorded the brothers' names on a list of all the members of their society, known as the One called Me.

"That ceremony means *something*," Terran said. "What could it be?"

When Zalcon returned Zoe to the compartment, the first officer told the trio, "I believe we now have all the information we need. However, it will still take a while to assimilate everything. In the meantime, you are now free to roam about the ship, so long as you in no way interfere with its operations."

"You mean," Zoe said incredulously, "we can just wander around and see whatever we like?"

"That is correct," said Zalcon.

"Perhaps," Eli said, "you could send someone to kinda show us around, so we don't get into trouble."

"Lieutenant Zane should be available," Zalcon said. "I'll see to it." And with that, he hurried out of the compartment, leaving the hatch open.

When Zoe was sure that Zalcon was out of earshot, he said, "Man, these alien kidnappers sure seem to be easygoing, all of a sudden."

"Yeah," said Eli, "these dudes are unbelievable. I'm as interested in them as they are in us."

"Me, too," said Bob. "I have a few questions I'd like answered myself. I still can't get over the fact that we're out here in orbit with these guys, who seem as normal as us." He took a step out into the passageway, looked around, and then stepped back in. "I only hope we can make it back home," he whispered. "At the moment, we don't have any control over our own fate."

This thought fanned the embers of their apprehension.

"All we can do," Eli said calmly, "is take it one minute at a time."

"You're right, Son. We've been in tight spots before, so let's just assume this one will turn out better than we can imagine."

Zoe and Eli smiled when they heard their father reiterate his favorite aphorism for dealing with dilemmas.

Still under the influence of the Smart Pills, Terran and his staff used their remaining time of enhanced focus to study the data and images they had collected.

"The Earthlings," Terran said, with another of his rare smiles, "are accomplishing for us the one part of this mission that we could never have achieved on our own..., recovering the time ship from the depths of the sea."

Mandoon cackled with delight. "According to our information," he said, "they may have already done so. Our intelligence tells us that the recovery effort to surface the craft was expected to take sixty days. Remember, it has been slightly more than seventy-two hours since we abducted the family. The trapezoidal effect of going back almost two hundred years into their past would translate into slightly more than two months by now."

Mandoon's statement should have sent a wave of excitement through the room, but Terran and the others were beginning to feel the diminishing effects of the mind enhancers, along with the fatigue from the past seventy-two hours.

"Lieutenant Zane," Zalcon said as he entered the bridge, "give the new prisoners the same tour we gave Rosario and Knox. You may answer any of their questions, but in no way are you to broach the subject of the crystals. We may need some more cooperation before we're through with them."

"At once, sir."

Back in the uneasy trio's compartment, although the hatch remained open, Bob and the boys had still not ventured out.

"Well?" asked Zoe. "What do you say? Are we gonna wait

for Lieutenant Zane to show up, or what? Maybe we should see what we can while we can."

"Okay," said Bob, "let's go!"

Just as they were leaving the compartment, Zane came around the corner.

II

The deep-sea endeavor had paid off. Two months and ten days after the placement of the first section of the Japanese flotation collar, the marvelous saucer was brought to the surface. The whole world rejoiced at this international achievement, and a surge of contentment swept over the planet. For the first time in history, all of humanity was truly at peace. The source of these universal feelings of brotherly love could not be explained in any other way than by the marvelous event at sea.

America was the first to proclaim this new worldwide spirit. "FAMILY OF MAN!" blared the headlines. Crimes and conflicts of every nature became irrelevant. Acts of selflessness and universal love became as commonplace as air and sunshine. Even military and law enforcement agencies turned their swords into plowshares, focusing their priorities on humanitarian services.

Still, there were some who were so consumed by their own greed that they were unaffected by the new wave of enlightenment. However, this minority was powerless in their objections because of overwhelming peer pressure.

The desire to further explore the contents of the alien craft became a global obsession. Although the entryway to the saucer was obvious, penetrating it was proving impossible. Even explosives failed to mar the craft's metallic skin.

There were many who wanted to leave well enough alone, contending that it was sufficient to reap the benefits of the saucer's presence, and that its impermeability should be respected. But there were others who passionately believed that they should persevere in trying to unlock the saucer's secrets.

"Gentlemen," said Zane, "I have been instructed to give you a tour of the areas of the ship that you may find interesting."

The trio was taken aback at the lieutenant's sudden appearance, but nonetheless put at ease by his amicable greeting.

Although Zane's invitation sounded promising, it was more of a ploy to relieve the prisoners' sense of confinement. Zane's orders were to keep them relaxed. His approach was working as they followed him down the blue-lit passageway.

Trying to take it all in as they passed by one perplexing workstation after another, Bob and the boys recognized none of the exotica that contributed to the ship's performance, and Zane offered no information about any of them.

"First," he said, "I'll show you where the galley is. You must be hungry after your sessions with Mandoon."

"Now that you mention it," Zoe said, "I am feeling a bit empty.... Tell me, Lieutenant Zane, where do you all come from? Surely not this solar system."

Bob's and Eli's eyebrows rose with Zoe's question, which seemed surreal. The fact that it was appropriate made the situation even more unnerving.

But Zane took the question in stride.

"Suffice it to say," he began, "we are from a place far, far away known as the Qwarzarian Galaxy. In your tiny solar system, the Earth is the only peopled planet. Where I come from, there are many peopled planets in a multitude of solar systems that are more or less just like yours. Our home is known as Marauda. It is the closest world to the cradle planet, Qwarz."

"Qwarz?" Zoe asked. "What's a cradle planet?"

"It is the original planet from which all the others in our galaxy were peopled. Qwarz is where the Garden of Eden was, and where the cradle race, the Lamorians, established another human race. All of the other planets of the Qwarzarian Galaxy are the descendants of Qwarz."

Astonished, Bob asked, "How can that be?"

"Now, *there's* something we have in common," Eli said. "We also have a Garden of Eden in our mythology..., the place on Earth where the first people appeared..., where our human race began..., Adam and Eve!"

Zane smiled condescendingly. "Isolated as you are in this tiny solar system, I am not surprised that you believe that you are the only humans in existence. But as I have already told you, that is not the case."

"We had no idea of any of this," Eli said. "Please, Lieutenant Zane, tell us more about the way things are."

"I can do better than that," Zane said, opening the hatch to a compartment on their left. "Step inside here."

Bob and the boys found themselves in a small room not more than ten feet by twelve. There were six stools fastened to the deck in a semicircle. In the center of this, there was a clear sphere not unlike the one they had seen on Mandoon's science deck. Next to one of the stools, there was an oblong stand with an indentation in the shape of a human hand at the top.

"Have a seat, gentlemen," Zane told them as he sat on the stool next to the stand, placing his hand into the indentation. The moment his hand touched the device, the large sphere lit up with what appeared to be a blue gaseous luminescence, holding the trio in rapt attention.

"That time ship you discovered," Zane said, "is a Lamorian craft, and proof that the cradle race chose your planet to propagate."

As he spoke, a holographic image of a saucer took shape within the sphere.

"That's the one!" said Zoe. "That's the one we found!"

"Or one just like it," said Zane. "In any case, it is no surprise to me that your mythology mentions a Garden of Eden. Legend tells us that approximately every one hundred thousand generations, a group of Lamorian pioneers venture into the endless night of space in search of a new sweet spot where conditions are just right to establish another garden planet. In this way, they continue the endless propagation of the cosmic seed known as mankind. In the infinite sea of space, we can only deduce that there was never a time when man was not. Consequently, we can assume there are countless numbers of undiscovered cradle planets. Yours is our latest discovery among several in the known galaxies."

"Our own astronomy," Bob said, "confirms the existence of other galaxies, but they are so far away that actually making contact with them seems utterly impossible to us. Obviously, you have the technology to travel those distances."

"The fact that I am standing here with you speaks for itself.... But, to continue, on Qwarz, in the Valley of Siniah, there are a number of indelible records etched on red marble tablets by a technique that is now a lost art."

As Zane spoke, images formed in the sphere that illustrated his words, holding the trio spellbound.

"*Jee*-zus!" Bob exclaimed. "We're looking at the Garden of Eden, boys!"

"Indeed," Zane said. "And the tablets you see undeniably verify the Lamorians' existence and illustrate their marvelous culture and stories through holographic images that appear every day when the sun shines on them."

All this while, Zane had not revealed the existence of the fabulous Esseen Crystals—or the robot empire, the Illuminosity, which ruled his galaxy.

"Any questions?" he asked.

Saturated with unfamiliar concepts, the Earthlings were

unable to think of anything.

"Alright," Zane said, "that's enough for now. Let's proceed to the galley."

Zane directed them to the food service units just inside the entry of the rectangular dining area. In contrast to everything else they had seen since leaving their quarters, the galley felt familiar.

Standing before what could only have been the Maraudians' version of a vending machine, Zane explained its function: "There is always food and drink available here. This button is for the *aubrice*." He was pointing to a rune-like symbol, which he now pressed.

A shiny metallic door lifted, allowing the selection to slide out—a concoction that resembled stew.

"That looks like what you gave us last night," Eli said.

"Yeah, my favorite," Zoe said sardonically.

"And, of course, there's always *catheequia*," Zane said, pressing the only other button.

This concoction resembled the first selection, but without gravy.

"I recommend the *aubrice* myself," said Zane, as he pushed three buttons on the drink dispenser. "Here we have cold water, and these two steaming ones are hot water and *danko*."

"I'll try the *danko*," said Bob. "It looks like coffee."

Picking up the cup of dark liquid, he passed it under his nose, but it had no aroma. He took a sip, and was immediately disappointed.

"It just tastes like hot water," he said. "What's the deal?"

"A cup of that," said Zane, "will keep you awake for hours. But two cups will put you out like a light."

When he heard that, Bob put down the cup. "On second thought," he said, "I'm not thirsty…. Or hungry, either."

"Same here," said Zoe.

"Yeah," said Eli.

Unphased, and eager to get his assignment over with, Zane said, "I suggest you take in the spacewalk next."

"Spacewalk?" Eli asked. "Do you mean we're actually going to walk out in space?"

Zane smiled. "The spacewalk is a breathtaking experience that will give you the *illusion* of walking on an observation deck outside the ship. But have no fear. You will still be within the ship's protective repellite hull."

"Sounds like a Disneyland attraction to me," Zoe said.

This comment brought a quizzical expression to Zane's face, but he said nothing as he started for the door at the opposite end of the dining hall. Following him, the trio noticed for the first time that the two men dressed like pirates were sitting at a table in a far corner, huddled over food. Bob nodded to them as he passed by, and they acknowledged him in kind.

"Who were those two in the galley?" Bob asked Zane when the group was ascending on another exposed elevator.

"A couple of pirates we are doing business with."

This answer was so evasive that Bob rolled his eyes as he looked at his sons.

Still awaiting their release from the Maraudians, Rosario and Knox were growing more anxious with each passing moment. Having been dragged along on yet another jaunt through time, they were rapidly losing hope that Terran would keep his promise to return them to the world and the life they had known.

With a scowl, as he tried to eat what could be his last meal, Knox said, "That dog Terran, 'e said 'e would let us go. I don't believe a word of it. And now, who are *these* three blokes? Terran seemed to think we might know 'em. Now that 'e's seen we 'aven't a clue, I'm afraid we might 'ave come to the end of our usefulness to 'im."

Rosario concurred: "Those three *must* be the reason Terran has kept us around till now…, and the Lieutenant never even gave us a glance as he went by. He knows something, says I."

Knox nodded. "Aye, Cap'n, more than *we* do, no doubt. Probably showin' 'em around the same way 'e did with us."

Rosario's brow rose with an idea. "I'm thinking those three are in the same boat as us…, and don't know it."

"Maybe we can find out somethin' from 'em, Cap'n."

"Anyway, we can tell them what we know, use them as allies. At least, we'll have us some mates to plan with."

"Aye, Cap'n, we can't be any worse off than we are now. Maybe we'll get lucky."

"We'll give them some time to start down the spacewalk, and then we'll catch up and see what they have to say."

The buccaneers had been in space a while now and, although they had not noticed, they were rapidly acclimating to its timeless effect. They referred to the spacewalk as if it were as common as the poop deck, rather than the astonishing place where they had first perceived the big picture of the Universe. Their daily routine aboard the *Maraudor* consisted of trips to the galley and listening to stories of conquest and plundering told them by crew members who, in spite of everything, seemed friendly enough. These experiences were transforming them into sailors of space, much like the Maraudians themselves. If it were not for their fear of being eliminated by Terran once they had served his purpose, they might have considered a career with the space pirates.

Returning to their lives back on the *Tortuga Diablo* after what they had seen and heard might not have been their first choice anymore, if plundering about the Universe with Terran's crew were an option. This idea had occurred to them on the few occasions that Terran's wrath seemed more remote—moments of denial, perhaps, but food for thought. But they always came back to the fact that they did not have anything to offer that would give the space pirates a reason to take them along.

Stepping off the elevator, the trio were captivated by a three-dimensional model on display next to a hatch that seemed to lead to the ship's exterior.

"What's that?" Bob asked.

"It's our ship," Zane replied. "The *Maraudor*."

"So, *that's* what this thing looks like!" Bob said in amazement.

Zoe and Eli stood speechless as they studied the model.

"We are here in the superstructure," Zane said. "The space-walk simulates what you would experience if you were to walk on the exterior from here all the way to the forward section. Of course, as I said, you will still be within the ship. I'm sure you will find the experience realistic."

"Looks like the superstructure's four stories high," said Zoe, still studying the model. "Judging from the size of the doors, it must be a good hundred yards from here to the bow. I wonder what that huge structure on the bow is all about. It kinda looks like the front end of a hammerhead shark."

"Those shields on each side make it look like a Viking long-boat," said Eli.

"They're not shields," said Zoe. "They're saucers. Can't you see their resemblance to the one we found in the water?"

"You're right, son," Bob said. "That's *exactly* what they are."

"Okay," said Eli, "those are saucers. But what are *these*?"

He was pointing to two mammoth circular housings protruding from the ship, one on each side, which resembled turbines.

The three of them looked to Zane for an explanation.

"I'm sorry, gentlemen," the Lieutenant announced, "but I have the next watch, and so I must leave you now. Whenever you are ready, you can go through this hatch and walk the length of the ship. You are free to continue your tour by yourselves. Ask anyone if you need assistance finding your way back to your quarters. Captain Terran will meet with you after your next sleep cycle. Until then, enjoy the experience."

Bob and the boys were disquieted to find themselves on their own as Zane took his leave, but said nothing as he ascended on the oval elevator.

"Well, what do you say?" Bob asked. "Shall we see what the spacewalk is all about?"

Both brothers shrugged.

The hatch they would have to pass through gave the illusion of leading directly into outer space—if indeed it *was* an illusion.

"This may be Terran's way of getting rid of us," Zoe said. "We just pop outside and *poof!* We're gone."

"That's just what *I* was thinking," Bob agreed, grimacing beneath furrowed eyebrows.

"If you're right, Zoe," Eli said, "we won't get a second chance once we open that hatch."

"Okay, boys, we'll forget the spacewalk, right?" Bob suggested. "But, on the other hand, if this hatch *does* open to outer space, how could that kind of exposure be tolerated by this interior? The vacuum would suck everything in *here* out *there!*"

"No matter what fantastic technology they may have," Eli said, "I don't see any airlocks around here, and those crew members and workstations over there would be floating icicles, just like us. Besides, I think they still need us.... Or at least they believe they do. I say we give it a try."

"I have to admit," Bob said, "Zane did sound sincere when he told us that Terran intended to meet with us after the next rest period."

"Yeah," Zoe agreed, "it wouldn't make sense to get rid of us now. We should be okay. Let's give it a shot."

He put his hand on the hatch release and looked at his father. Bob nodded. "Go for it!"

Zoe hit the release, causing the oval hatch to roll away to one side. To their relief, there was no change in pressure, no drop in temperature, and no loss of air—confirming that they were still within the ship.

They stepped out into the surreal. Enthralled by the seamless simulation, they felt as if they were standing in the depths of outer space.

As the hatch rolled shut, they looked up at the ship's superstructure towering over them. The Earth was suspended off the port bow, looking like a giant blue marble. On the starboard side, the silver grey moon floated beneath them.

Zoe stood transfixed. "Man, that moon is *close!* You could almost touch it."

"I feel so small," Bob said. "Like a speck of consciousness floating in space."

"Yeah, this is awesome," said Eli. "It makes the trip worth it..., I hope."

Mesmerized, they continued on in silence. But as they reached the middle of the hundred yard trek, they saw two figures approaching them.

"Look!" Zoe said. "It's those two pirates from the galley."

"Yeah, that's right!" said Eli. "Rosario and Knox."

"According to the doctor's report," Bob reminded them, "we knew these guys before. Now we're back together *out here*. What can all this mean? Let *them* do the talking. They don't know who we are. Let's see what's on their minds."

"Ahoy, mates! We would 'ave words with you. My name's Will Knox, and this 'ere's Cap'n Rosario. We were wonderin' if ya know about these space dogs you're dealin' with…, and if you're prisoners 'ere like us."

When Bob and the boys heard these words, chills ran down their spines.

Trying not to focus on Rosario's disturbing wide-eyed glare, Bob answered, "I guess you could say we're prisoners. We were kidnapped, and woke up aboard this ship."

Both pirates nodded.

"Terran is indeed a treacherous one," Rosario said, his warm tone contradicting his eerie façade. "He's after your gold, no doubt, trying to find out where you've hidden it."

"I'm not sure *what* he's after," Bob said, trying to shrug off his queasiness. "But as for gold, we have none."

The buccaneers looked at each other in disbelief, surprised to hear there was no gold at stake.

As Eli and Zoe tried to make sense of all this, they could not stop staring at Rosario's crazed expression.

"No gold!" Knox exclaimed. "Well, there be *somethin'* you've got that 'e wants, to be sure."

"Whatever it is," growled Rosario, "your lives won't be worth an ounce of wet powder after he gets it. Lost most of my crew, I did, to that blackguard. Over two hundred men went down to Davy Jones. Mister Knox here and myself are all that's left, and it won't be long before *we're* gone, too…, unless we can figure a way out."

The trio listened anxiously to Rosario's dire words. The more they considered their predicament, the more hopeless it seemed.

"If you're right," Eli said, "and I don't doubt you are, what can we do about it? We're out in space on a ship we can't navigate even if we *could* take it over."

A row of wrinkles furrowed across Rosario's forehead. "It's true," he said, "we're helpless as long as we remain prisoners here. Terran promised to return us to our ship, the *Tortuga Diablo*, when he's through with you three, but we don't believe he will."

These words made Bob's forehead furrow as well. "Where *is* the *Tortuga Diablo*, Captain?" he asked.

Knox answered for Rosario: "She's back in the Bay of Turtle Island by now, to be sure. We were tryin' to get away, makin' for the Northern Wilds, when they came for us. Cap'n Pizzo, the first mate, would have returned to Tortuga by now. There's no use tryin' to run from these blokes. They can find us, no matter where we are."

"That can only mean one thing," said Zoe. "We must be lost in time again! Tell me, Captain, what year was it when they took you prisoner?"

Rosario and Knox looked at each other anxiously. "It was no more than three weeks ago," the captain said. "Eighteen-nineteen it is…, although where we are now we can't say." Noting the trio's crestfallen reaction, he continued, "Time is like another ocean to these space pirates. They can travel forward or backward in time as easy as sailing from one island to the next. I lost my crew when they sent us back a hundred years to fetch Blackbeard's gold. We returned with only a few survivors…and me with this terrible misshapenness branded on my face. There's no reason to think they'll set us free. If they do, it'll be the first time ever, to be sure!"

The captain's awareness of how he looked quelled the idea that he was a madman, but the message he bore was one of almost certain doom.

"We must put our heads together," Bob said, "to come up with a way to outsmart these space dogs and escape their grasp."

"Our only chance," replied Rosario, "would be to make them think we still have something they can use…, something to buy us time until we can turn the tables on them."

"Agreed, Captain!" Bob said. "It would probably be in everyone's best interest," he added, looking at his sons, "to tell these gentlemen all we know about Doctor Dave's report."

The boys nodded.

"Captain Rosario," Bob said, turning back to the buccaneers, "it seems we knew each other somewhere back in time…, and now, as a result of that occurrence, these space pirates have brought us together again."

Brett had been a member of the paintball family operation since he was eleven years old. Now, at twenty-five, he was the field manager as well as a trusted confidant who knew every aspect of the business.

"Whatever happened," he would say, "I know we haven't heard the last of them. I'll just keep it all going until they return."

That was his stock answer to every inquiry, including those made by federal special agents Brock and Hess, who stopped by every two weeks to ask the same questions about the circumstances surrounding that fateful day.

Eight weeks had come and gone since Brett had become the full-time manager of Paintball Jungle—two months since Bob and his sons had mysteriously disappeared in the middle of the action on the paintball field.

The American Canyon Police Department, typically a humdrum outpost in the world of crime, was hard-pressed having to deal with two abductions on the same day. The first was the case of two bewildered paintball sportsmen who came staggering into the police station, claiming they had been kidnapped.

"We don't know, Officer," said one of them, "what exactly happened. We were the first to arrive at the Jungle this morning. As we were preparing our equipment in the parking lot, six or seven people approached us on foot. We thought they were fellow paintballers, but wondered how they had gotten there, since there were no other cars in the lot. They must have knocked us out somehow, because the next thing we knew, it was afternoon and we found ourselves about a mile away, next to our SUV. We weren't robbed and, except for feeling confused and unsteady on our feet when we came to, we have nothing else to tell you."

While taking their statements, the police had been skeptical of their story until later that afternoon, when Brett reported that the field owner and his two sons were missing. This second disappearance was obviously foul play, since their expensive guns and ammo packs were found on the playing field where they had been. Subsequently, the mysterious case caught the attention of the state and federal authorities and, ultimately, the FBI. After eight weeks, the incident still remained a mystery.

The facts of the story had not changed since Brett made his initial statement.

"Come to think of it," he had reported, "there was a suspicious player named Mike Kelly, who came here in a white SUV. He said he was a reporter for the *Chronicle* and started asking questions about Bob, Eli, and Zoe. We thought the questions were odd, but we answered them just the same."

The liability waiver signed by Kelly confirmed these details, although the *Chronicle* denied having a Michael Kelly on its staff. There seemed to be a link between the two cases, however, since a white SUV was involved in both of them. But, aside from these sparse clues, nothing else had been discovered, leaving everyone perplexed as to what could have become of Magic Carpet Bob, Eli, and Zoe.

The *Maraudor* was still orbiting Earth in the year 1890 while the staff assimilated their newly gathered intelligence. After leaving Bob and the boys on the spacewalk, Zane returned to the bridge, where he found Terran in a heated discussion with Mandoon and Zalcon. The science officer was concerned about the many recent time spikes they had caused, in addition to the ominous spike that came from the Lamorians. He was worried that these would reveal their present location to their nemesis, the all-powerful Illuminosity.

"If they find us," he said, "I'm sure you know it won't go easy for us."

The elevated tone of his voice indicated that the space wizard was quite agitated.

"I concur, Captain," said Zalcon. "We may already have gone too far. We must be on the lookout for them and be prepared to flee at a moment's notice."

"We cannot stop now," Terran said bluntly. "We must stay our course. We are close to obtaining the crystals, and nothing shall deter us. As for the Illuminosity, we have always kept three steps ahead of those robots, and we will continue to do so now."

Ever since he had confirmed the existence of the Lamorian time ship, Terran had become obsessed with possessing the fabulous Esseen Crystals at any cost. Many times in the past, his officers had seen their notorious captain in this state over his insatiable lust for gold, but this latest case of extreme tunnel vision was unprecedented. The captain had transcended into the Maraudian state of ruthless greed known as the Rapture.

"Captain," Zane said, "Rosario and Knox are on the spacewalk, talking to the other three at this moment."

"What does that matter?" Terran said with a wave of his hand. "All I care about is the crystals. Once we have those aboard, we'll jettison the Earthlings along with the rest of the garbage and be on our way. We need to get back to the future as soon as the time ship is brought to the surface, so we can board her and seize the crystals."

The officers knew that Terran's Rapture was well beyond debate. Now it was a matter of following orders and hoping for the best.

"We might as well go in shooting," said Zalcon.

"Right you are," Terran agreed. "A surprise attack, quick and to the point."

"Captain," Mandoon said, "although we have been away only a short while, when we return to the future from here, six to eight weeks will have elapsed from the time we left because of the trapezoidal effect of time travel. We'll need to go into orbit and get caught up on what progress has been made on Earth before we can further plan our reinsertion."

Terran gave the space wizard a brief smile. "Now you're on track, Mandoon," he said. "Let's stay focused on the objective. Nothing else matters."

All this time, Bob and the boys had been telling Rosario and Knox everything they knew about their experiences back on the island where the Lamorians had marooned them in time.

"As far as I can tell," Bob said, "this all began when my boys and I discovered a sunken saucer off the coast of Bermuda."

"Aye," said Rosario, "the place they used to call the Isle of

Devils."

"Hmmm, that's true..., I hadn't thought of that. Anyway, aside from finding that spaceship..., and we have pictures of that..., I can't say that I remember any of those events. But I do believe the doctor who told me these things."

"Your story is unbelievable," said Rosario. "How you could know about the *Tortuga Diablo*, let alone my men..., Joaquin, Villa, and Wilkes..., I cannot fathom. That you do speaks of a common cause between us. One thing remains sure. We are all in the hands of a strange and powerful enemy, and our only chance now is to work together to solve our plight."

"However, Captain," Bob said, "standing here and talking about these things can only harm our cause."

"Right you are," Rosario said. "We can't let them think that they have anything to worry about from us. As long as we're permitted to move about the ship freely, we have a chance. If they confine us to quarters, we're sunk."

"We'd better break this little meeting up," said Zoe.

"That's right," said Eli. "They could be watching us or listening to us at this very moment."

"Let's all return to quarters," Bob said, "and try to meet again after our next sleep cycle."

"Aye, we'll go back the way we came," Knox said. "And we'll meet later in the galley. Until then, let's try to come up with an idea for our next move."

"I don't know, honey," said Suzanne Wong as she viewed her fiancé on the screen of her laptop. "I just don't feel the same way about all of this."

"Yeah, baby," answered Gary Grogan. "I know what you mean. Ever since they brought that saucer to the surface, I've been having second thoughts about the spin we've been putting on this whole deal."

"At first, I was so confused," Suzanne said. "But now I'm sure that I can no longer fan the fires of sensationalism with this."

"Me, too," said Gary. "And it's not just us. Everyone I talk to around here seems to be second-guessing about what they're doing with their lives."

Suddenly, the intercom broke up the conversation.

"Miss Wong," the voice of authority demanded, "get in here now!"

"Yes, Mr. Rupert," she said, "I'm on my way." Turning back to the screen, she said, "Honey, I've gotta go. He called me Miss Wong, and you know what *that* means."

Without bothering to sign off, she raced down the hall to the wide oak door that read "Murray Rupert, President."

"He's waiting for you, Suzanne," said the receptionist. "Go right in."

Suzanne closed the door of the inner office behind her and braced for the obvious explosion about to erupt from the red-faced mogul seated at his desk.

"What the hell's goin' on around here?" he began. "Is everybody going out of their bloody minds?"

Knowing exactly what he was referring to, she feigned a puzzled expression as she said, "I'm sorry, sir, but I'm not quite following you."

"Oh, *really*, Miss Wong!" he shot back. "I'm even starting to wonder about *you*. I'm talking about the obvious lack of enthusiasm by everyone around here about the threat the alien craft poses to America and the whole world! I gave strict orders to spin this story as a grave threat to global security. I told you that I wanted the paranoid angle on this expanded. I want the U.S. Navy to look like they're the only ones on top of the problem, and all the others to look like bumbling idiots."

"Yes, Mr. Rupert," Suzanne said sheepishly.

"Yeah, well, ever since they brought that thing to the surface, all I've been hearing out of everybody are namby-pamby diatribes about love and peace. This whole thing is breaking down! If this goes on, we'll all be out of a job. We can't make any money on world peace…, nobody can. If you want to stay in that palace you call home up there in Fairview, you had better get on the stick."

"Now that you mention it, boss," she said, trying to buffer the jagged edges of his mood, "I *have* noticed a change in the air."

"Yes," Rupert said. "Well, I just got off the phone with President Ivy. He's furious. Says he's already lost half of his team up on the hill. They're just quitting, dropping off like flies. We've never had a problem like this. It's the *Martian Chronicles* for real. Those aliens are hypnotizing us, I tell you!"

Suzanne had seen her boss upset and angry over issues on many occasions, but never raging like this. There was real fear and desperation in his voice.

"When you go on the air tonight," he said, glaring at his nightly news anchorwoman, "I want the whole hour focused on this problem. We've got to turn this madness around before we all lose the fortunes we've amassed..., or even worse, money won't mean anything. It'll be worthless, along with everything else we hold near and dear. Get your writers in line. I want some real meaningful editorials tonight. Your job's at stake. Now, get out there!"

"Okay, boss."

As she made her way back to her office, her mind was racing.

My job's at stake, he says. Well, I'm having second thoughts about this job, Mister Murray Rupert. Greedy bastard! All you can think about is your money. I'll admit, I was like that, too. But now I realize there are more important things than money. I'm sick of this party line. All the little people and their problems are what's important. If I can't use my airtime to try to make things better, and to try to make up for all the damage I've done in the past, then a parting of the ways is in store for me and Vox News.

That night, Suzanne Wong's lead story was about the effect the saucer was having on the local scene, as well as the world.

"There are some," she stated, "who claim that the alien craft is somehow controlling our minds. It's the end of civilization as we know it, they say. We must destroy the craft before it destroys us!"

Murray Rupert's eyebrows rose, wrinkling his forehead.

"What's she saying?" he asked himself aloud as he sat watching the screen in his office alone.

"Well, it seems to me," she continued, "that civilization was well on its way to destroying itself long before the alien craft was discovered. In my hand, I have more than a dozen reports of unprecedented instances that are being attributed to the presence of the alien craft since it was surfaced." Wong held up one of the sheets of paper in her hand. "From Russia," she went on, "it's being reported that the many orphanages of that country are all but empty as the number of applications for adoptions are exceeding the number of wards of the state. And this one from Steven Weeks, the director of the California Humane Society, reports that there are no homeless pets anywhere in the state. Every dog, cat, and rabbit has been adopted, and now there's a waiting list. Our own traffic reporter, Wendy Hall, tells us that there's no traffic anywhere, since people are using the public transportation services in record numbers."

Suzanne kept the stories coming, one after another, of people everywhere performing acts of kindness and selflessness. "Yesterday," she said, "was cleanup day on the state beaches. All along the coast, droves of people combed the beaches, removing every bit of trash and debris. All I can say about those who claim that the alien influence is meant to destroy us is that people who choose to believe that have no common sense. To this reporter, it's as plain as the nose on my face that ever since the alien craft was surfaced, the whole world is becoming a much better place…, better than it's ever been. In closing tonight's show, I would just like to thank all of you and apologize for any misinformation I may have reported in the past. I'm sure my boss, Murray Rupert, will have some special words for me after tonight…. So this is Suzanne Wong saying, Goodnight, goodbye, and God bless."

There was no doubt about it—the world had become a wonderful place since the saucer was surfaced. The sea dock was like a cosmic fireplace, emanating its benevolent influence to all the corners of the Earth. No one could have guessed that it would come to symbolize the unification of the peoples of the Earth. Floating peacefully on the high seas, housing the alien craft within its spacious perimeter, it had taken on the air of a temple.

Simultaneously with Wong's last broadcast, reporters all over the world were telling of countless incidents of man's humanity to man, instead of the normal horror stories that had always dominated the news. A miraculous surge of health and well-being was sweeping the globe. Except for maternity wards, hospitals literally emptied out. The famous brotherly love movement of the late 1960s paled in comparison to what was now taking place as people everywhere acknowledged the Family of Man.

President Ivy took to the airwaves every night before the six o'clock news. "My fellow Americans," he began, as he always did, "we are in troubled times. There has never before been an invasion attempt such as the world now faces. It is plain to see that the alien craft is somehow attempting to neutralize the very fabric of civilization. We must resist this at any cost and see it for the hideous threat it is. As I speak, my administration is organizing an attack on the sea dock and its tenant. We must obliterate the saucer here and now. While preparations are under way to do that, I implore you to remain firm and reject any ideas of alternatives to our plan of attack!"

Ivy's efforts to suppress any information about what was really happening were to no avail. Only the dwindling minority of self-serving powermongers, whose all-consuming greed kept them immune to the new awakening of human spirit, paid any attention to his diatribes of paranoia. But after rigging elections, waging war under false pretenses, and stifling opposition to their wholesale dismantling of a once-thriving democracy, those misanthropes were now reduced in ranks to the few villainous hangers-on who directly profited from their own nefarious policies. Each day, there were more and more instances of people flatly refusing to carry out negative directives against the better interests of mankind and the environment.

Bob and the boys returned to their quarters heavy-hearted. Their conference with the buccaneers had brought out their worst fears.

With instincts that had been honed over many years by a

series of marathon survival courses and a career of professional paintball, Zoe knew that when he felt his core burning hot with anticipation of the unknown, something was about to strike.

"If what they're telling us is true," he said, "we can forget about ever getting back home. Terran's promise of a happy ending when he's through with us doesn't seem likely after he's already wiped out most of Rosario's crew. Just the fact that he kidnapped us off the planet proves what he's capable of. Let's face it…, we're in big trouble!"

"Man," said Eli, "we've *gotta* figure a way out of this, and it doesn't feel like we have much time. Here in space, we're powerless. We must convince Terran that he still needs us to accomplish his business on Earth, whatever that may be. We'll never get a chance to escape until we're back on land."

Sitting on his bunk, Bob listened with his head in his hands. In a rare moment, the consummate optimist had no idea how to proceed. One thing was for sure—the future looked bleak.

"Well, I'm getting hungry," Eli said. "What do you say we get some of that rocket ship stew? Maybe we'll feel more creative after we eat, or maybe we'll see something we can use to make a plan."

"Right, let's go!" Bob said, seizing the suggestion like a life preserver in a sea of pessimism.

One deck below the trio's, Rosario and Knox were scheming in their quarters. Ever since the first day that Terran had entered their lives, the buccaneers had been plotting to defeat the space pirate. That they had not yet come up with a working plan for how to accomplish this did not dampen their belief that they would ultimately succeed. At this moment, they were trying to devise a way to commandeer one of the space barges, along with Mandoon and the time portal.

"It should be no different than commandeering *any* ship," Rosario said. "Of course, the first thing we'll need is weapons."

"Aye, Cap'n," Knox answered, "and that's our first deadlock. These devils use weapons the likes of which we've never seen..., let alone know 'ow to use."

Rosario grimaced but said nothing.

"Even if we do learn 'ow to use their weapons," Knox continued, "we'll need able bodies to man that flyin' machine of theirs."

"I'll admit," said Rosario, "it's a lot to get done by blokes who never dreamed such things even existed."

"Right, Cap'n, and from what they say, I don't think Bob and his sons ever saw the rig that brought 'em 'ere..., or the time contraption."

"Yes, there are many things about these space dogs that Bob and his sons don't seem to know, to be sure. We'll have to explain it to them."

"Aye, Cap'n, if there's one thing they *do* know, it's that these space dogs won't think twice when it's time to cast off the lot of us."

In the mess hall, as the trio reluctantly ate their space vittles, they were disappointed that Rosario and Knox were not there. On the walk back to their compartment, Bob and the boys studied the various workstations along the way, hoping to gain some inspiration for their escape. But there was nothing they could recognize, let alone use for their purpose. When they returned to their bunks, dismal desperation had overtaken them as, one by one, they fell off to sleep.

The bridge of the *Maraudor* was alive with preparations to make the jump from 1890 to 2006.

"Mandoon," Terran snapped, "be quick! I want to get underway."

"Yes, Captain. Another moment or two and we'll be off."

"Carry on. It can't be too soon for me."

"If I may, sir," Zalcon interjected, "there is one detail that would cause irreparable damage if overlooked."

"What is it, then?" Terran demanded without looking up at his first officer.

"Captain, we must make sure the prisoners are in proper position for the leap."

Without acknowledging his oversight, the captain turned to Zane. "Make no mistake," he said. "Give Rosario and the other one notice of our intentions, but make sure you stay with the trio until we have completed the jump. I don't want there to be any chance of them being maimed before they have served their purpose. Make it so."

"At once, Captain," said Zane as he hastened off to follow his orders.

The trio awoke as soon as the hatch rolled open.

"Gentleman," Zane said, stepping into the compartment,

"I'm sorry to disturb you, but it will be necessary for all of you to stand and face the hatchway, keeping your eyes straight ahead. We are about to travel to your time period, and maintaining that position is essential for your safe return."

Without a word, the trio stood, following the lieutenant's instructions.

Speaking into a device on his wrist, Zane said, "Captain, all is ready here."

A cracking flash of white light followed the acknowledgment from the bridge.

"It is done, gentlemen," said Zane. "You may relax now."

"I must speak to the captain at once," Bob said.

"I'm sorry," Zane answered, "but now is not a good time. The captain is very busy at the moment, but I'm sure you'll be hearing from him before long."

With that, Zane returned to the bridge, leaving the hatch open.

As soon as the *Maraudor* made the jump into the next temporal corridor, all of her data-compiling equipment searched for information about the present status of the prize. Within a few hours, Terran's crew began to understand the situation on the planet. Apparently, the recovery team had surfaced the saucer several weeks before. While there was a noticeable absence of the usual military communications that had always been present on their previous orbits, the Internet was buzzing with interest about the Lamorian time ship and the sea dock. Evidently, all attempts to enter the craft had failed. Nevertheless, praise of the new wonderful sense of well-being was coming from all points of the globe.

"It must be the crystals," Mandoon said, "that are causing the Earthlings to rise above their petty squabbles."

"Yes," said Zalcon, "that would explain it. Even though none of us have ever had any direct experience with these mythical jewels, I, too, believe that this fervor sweeping the planet can only be the result of the legendary crystals."

"Most extraordinary effect," said Terran, "given that the crystals are still sealed within the time ship. I wonder what effect the Esseen crystals will have on *us* once they are in our hands."

Everyone on the bridge fell silent, contemplating their captain's words.

"Agh!" Terran snarled. "All that matters is that we possess the most sought-after prize in the Universe. These Earthlings are not like us.... They are weak. We are Pirates of Marauda..., bold, strong cosmic adventurers. These are the qualities that will be enhanced in us, just as peace and love were enhanced in those pitiful Earthlings. Yes! There is nothing to fear! Make ready. Our greatest fortune is waiting for us. We have but to go and take it."

Deep in the Rapture, Terran was becoming more frantic with each new revelation. Together with his staff, he pored over the data about the time ship. Aside from the writings and holograms from Qwarz, the rest of what the Maraudians knew about the craft came from the sessions with the Hat.

"If the Earthlings cannot get into the saucer," Zalcon said, "*we* may have the same problem. After all, we know very little about Lamorian shipbuilding."

"We do know," said Terran, "that their spaceships were engineered to only allow Lamorians to operate them."

"Perhaps," said Mandoon, "there is a clue in the lock of hair. Remember? When Bob's sons were back on the island, the Lamorians took a lock of their hair before adding their names to the scroll of the One called Me."

"What could be the significance of such a ceremony?" Terran wondered aloud. "Why would such a requirement be necessary?"

While Terran was pondering this, Bob and his sons were searching for Rosario and Knox.

As they cautiously proceeded through the empty passageway, Zoe said softly, "We need a plan. Whatever we're gonna do, we've gotta do it *soon.*

Instinctively, Bob held his finger to his lips and then pointed to the mess hall. "We'll check there first," he said, "and then the spacewalk. Maybe we'll get lucky."

When the buccaneers were not at the mess hall, the trio hastened to the spacewalk, where they found their confederates waiting.

"We're back in *your* time, mates," Rosario said. "They've come back here again for reasons only *they* know."

"I think *I* know why they're here," Bob said. "I bet they're gonna try to do something about that saucer we discovered. What they have in mind I can't say, but I'm sure the saucer's at the bottom of all of this."

Rosario and Knox heard Bob's words, but could not begin to grasp their meaning.

"Well, be that as it may," Rosario said, "we still have *our* problems to solve. We're halfway to a plan, but first we were wondering if you knew about their sky barges and their time device…, the things they brought you here in and what they use to travel through time as they do."

As Rosario mentioned these alien devices, Bob and his sons listened in amazement.

"This sky barge you describe," Bob said, "sounds like the saucer we discovered."

"Aye," said Knox, "it's all startin' to make sense now."

"We're of a mind," said Rosario, "to take the one called Mandoon and his time machine, then commandeer a sky barge and make our escape. Just how we can arrange these things is the part of the plan we haven't figured out yet."

Bob looked at Eli and Zoe, rolling his eyes. "Sounds like *less* than half a plan to me," he said. "You must admit, there are some major parts of that puzzle still missing, Captain."

"Agreed," said Rosario, undaunted, "but come along. We'll show you where they keep the sky barge docked. Between us, we'll think of something, I'm sure of it."

While the trio had not seen this part of the ship yet, any plan they might execute would have to include a familiarity with the hangar deck.

Rosario's idea seemed ridiculous to Bob, but he appreciated the man's optimism.

"Very well, Captain," he said, "lead on."

Immersed in the throes of the Rapture, the Maraudians were totally focused on the problem of gaining entry into the saucer. Pressed by Terran to come up with the solution, Mandoon was hot on the trail, surmising that what they were looking for was within the data they had already compiled.

"That's *it!*" the wizard shouted suddenly, startling Terran and the others.

"*What's* it?" demanded the captain. "What are you seeing that we missed?"

Turning to face his commander, Mandoon cackled in his maniacal tone. "The One called Me!" he said. "*That's* the key!"

Whatever the wizard was talking about escaped the rest of the team as they stared at him, waiting for an explanation.

"*That's* what the hair was for," Mandoon said. "Their DNA! The Lamorians referred to it. We saw it in the sessions with the Hat. Remember? They said the ship can only be entered by the One called Me. That would include the two sons. They were inducted in that ceremony, so they must be capable of entering the time ship."

Terran's eyes glazed over as a devilish grin broke across his usual stern expression. "Well done, Commander," he said. "I believe we now have all we need to reach our objective. It's still not clear exactly how we will apply the prisoners' DNA to gain entry, but I am confident that you have indeed found the key. It might be as simple as standing them in front of the hatch..., or maybe the craft is voice activated. We will figure it out. Commander Zalcon, prepare the barge for immediate departure. Commander Mandoon, install the time portal. We will go back to the exact coordinates of the sea dock in the year 1890 and then jump forward to make an instantaneous appearance. Catching them by surprise will afford us our best opportunity to board and stun everyone before they know what is happening."

"Yes, Captain!" they responded in unison.

"Lieutenant Zane, bring the brothers to the hangar deck. Leave the father behind. That will ensure their cooperation."

"At once, Captain," Zane said, nodding.

When it came to the *Maraudor*, the old saying that the walls have ears was accurate. Although the Earthlings never suspected it, there was not a single spoken word among them that went undetected. The Maraudians were well aware of their half-baked schemes for escape. However, given the captives' hopeless situation, these plans were of little concern to the space pirates.

Lieutenant Zane found the trio in their quarters. Standing between the brothers and facing Bob, he said, "The captain requires your sons' presence on the hangar deck. You, sir, will remain here."

Zane's orders and his cold tone sent a jagged wave of fear through Bob as he jumped to his feet. "Where are you taking my boys?" he demanded. "Why am I not going, too?"

"I have no idea," Zane said. "The captain does not consult

with me when he gives orders.... You two, follow me!"

Smiling, Zoe said, "It's okay, Dad, we'll be right back."

Bob looked at his boys and smiled grimly. He did not like the sound of this, but there was nothing he could do about it.

Eli and Zoe said nothing more as they followed the lieutenant out of the compartment, leaving their father to an uneasy solitude.

Terran was going over some plans with Zalcon when Eli and Zoe came aboard the sky barge.

"Prepare the prisoners for immediate departure," he said, shooting them a fiery glare. "I am well aware of your plans to commandeer this sky barge, along with my science officer and the time portal. In fact, there is not a word you have spoken on the *Maraudor* that I have not heard. Now, only your complete cooperation will ensure your father's safety..., as well as your own. Let there be no misunderstanding about *that*."

When the boys heard that they had been discovered, their hearts sank. Terran's cold-blooded words overwhelmed them with the harsh realization of his ruthless intentions.

"We'll do whatever it takes to keep our father safe, Captain," Eli said. "You can be sure of that."

Turning to Zane, Terran barked out his next order: "Alright, let's be on our way!"

As soon as Eli and Zoe were shown where to stand and how to focus their gaze, the craft rocked and separated from the mother ship. When Terran nodded to Mandoon, there was a flash of white light as they made the jump back through time. They were now hovering over the coordinates, two hundred miles off the northwest coast of Bermuda, precisely where the sea dock would be when they returned to the twenty-first century.

Eli and Zoe were now feeling the stark hopelessness of their plight. Making plans with Rosario and Knox had been doomed from the start, and now, even if they could somehow manage to separate from the Maraudians once they were back in their own time, they would never desert their father.

The *Maraudor* was one of many star cruisers built on the Illuminosity's home planet of Ulantia. The Ulantians were the only ones that the robot empire permitted to manufacture the marvelous repellite-hulled galactic cruisers. The built-in all-seeing-and-hearing sensory faculties of the *Maraudor* were a powerful component in the ship's design. Terran always assumed that this feature was intended to enable the captain to be aware of everything that transpired within his command. In fact, there was not a ship in the whole Qwarzarian Galaxy that did not contain this covert monitoring system. The feature was not optional.

The robots' prime directive, set forth by their now-extinct human creators, was to harvest intelligence in all forms and gold at any cost. They achieved this by controlling the manufacturing of space cruisers and selling them only to those who were worthy of command—namely, those who had attained the title of Pirates of Marauda.

However, as clever a spy as Terran had been with his captives, he was himself a victim of spying on an even greater scale. He never imagined that, in addition to the covert monitoring system that he controlled, there was an omniscient tracking device that knew precisely where he was—and when—as well as everything that was done and said aboard his ship. This device was deeply embedded in every Ulantian craft, undetectable by anyone or anything other than the robots themselves.

Of the nearly five hundred Maraudian pirate commanders, all of whom were free to plunder the galaxies, Terran had distinguished himself as the wiliest and most intrepid of them all. It was for this reason that the robots regarded him and his crew as their primary guinea pigs for testing their latest inventions. Terran never suspected that the Empire was constantly monitoring his exploits. The surface scanners, the Smart Pills, the mind reader known as the Hat, and, most recently, the time portal, all of which Terran had always thought he had stolen with the help of paid informants, had actually been deliberately fed to him by double agents.

But now he had gone too far. His discovery of the Esseen Crystals demanded an extraordinary response. The robots could no longer continue the guise as Terran's dupes. The vast annals of the Empire's ongoing harvest of intelligence contained the legends, fables, and all else that was known about the most sought-after jewels of the Universe. The legends promised longevity and the "powers of the gods" to anyone who possessed the crystals—reason enough to curtail Terran's adventure before he succeeded in acquiring the ultimate prize. The Esseen Crystals were just as highly valued by the robots as by the humans, but for a very different reason, namely, to keep them out of human hands.

The Illuminosity produced their own time spike, which sent their starship across the ocean of space to the newly discovered Milky Way Galaxy to seize the *Maraudor* and terminate Terran's tour of unbridled plundering.

Only a few ships remained around the sea dock, where there had been no less than fifty when the saucer was first surfaced. As the subsequent days turned into weeks, most of the expeditionary forces had returned to their ports. All that remained at the site were a few of the original personnel, including the recently demoted submarine captain, Robert Walsh of the *San Francisco*, the SRDRS that had been lost in the effort to retrieve the Lamorian time ship. He was now the newly appointed director of operations for the sea dock. The demotion was meant to be an insult to the old sea dog, who was known for the many adventures he had been part of in the submarine service. But Captain Walsh was actually delighted with his demotion. Instead of carrying out the tyrannical missions of the current administration, he now spent his days peacefully maintaining the seagoing shelter for the marvelous saucer.

There had been several TV interviews with Walsh, in which

he always made the same point. In the last one, he said, "Maintaining the support system for this awesome craft is an honor and the duty of people like myself, who have always dedicated their lives to serving humanity."

Walsh was a changed man. He and his staff had no desire to leave their miraculous find. Devoted to the project, they now spent their time vigilantly servicing the sea dock. Because of the saucer's mystical vibrations, this new, normally mundane duty was what Walsh considered the pinnacle of his illustrious career. He was more than content to be the caretaker of the alien craft, with its inexplicable influences that were the source of such great satisfaction to him and his men. Since gaining entry to the time ship was now considered futile, the only visitors now were occasional supply ships.

One day aboard the sea dock, as a warm breeze gently rocked the alien temple over a peaceful sea, Terran's sky barge suddenly appeared out of nowhere, hovered for a moment, and then landed. Sitting at his desk, Walsh could hardly believe his eyes as the alien craft set down on the heliport opposite his second-floor office window. His shock lasted only an instant before his well-honed reflex slammed into action. As the intruders came running down the ramp into the interior of the sea dock, Walsh scrambled to send an all-points alert.

A dozen of the staff were startled when Terran's away team burst through the entry and stunned them where they stood. In the second-floor communications room, Walsh and three crew members managed to get off a cry for help before they, too, were neutralized.

"The sea dock is under attack..., alien craft..., SOS!"

However, the compelling call for assistance was received by what had now become a lackadaisical response network, a result of the new priorities spawned by the crystals.

Right behind the assault team, Mandoon and two troops were hurrying Eli and Zoe down the ramp toward the sea dock. Despite everything that was happening, at the moment the boys entered the structure they were overwhelmed by the familiar feeling of well-being—the very same they had experienced the year before when they first discovered the saucer deep in the Bermuda Triangle.

The Maraudians did not share this euphoria because their single-minded greedy obsession to possess the prize kept them immune to the saucer's power.

When Mandoon arrived with the others at the sealed entrance of the time ship as it rocked gently within its moorings, he immediately spotted the hand-shaped indentation next to the hatch. Surmising what it was for, he placed his hand on it, but nothing happened. His eyebrow rose. Mumbling to himself, "We are all the one called me," he had a sudden insight. "Captain," he said, turning to Terran, "have one of the brothers place his left hand here as I have just done."

Terran jerked Eli into position. "Your left hand..., there..., now!"

Eli put his hand on the indentation. Immediately, there was a loud clink as the hatch rolled to one side.

Startled by their success, they all gazed into the ancient bronze-colored interior, which was indirectly lit by an amber glow. There were five decks accessed by an ascending ramp.

"Looks like something out of Jules Verne," Zoe said reverently. "Like the *Nautilus*."

As they all entered the craft, even the Maraudians were engulfed in waves of enlightenment. The rapacious space pirates could no longer resist the miraculous effect of the Esseen Crystals.

III

Aboard the *Maraudor*, the crew stood ready to leave orbit as soon as Terran and the away team returned with the fabulous prize. On the bridge, the subtle sounds emanating from the array of instruments that ran the great star cruiser confirmed that all was well.

Suddenly, an alarm sounded from the tracking station, indicating that a time spike had just occurred. In the same instant, an intruder appeared off the port bow.

"Intruder alert!" barked Chief Mazor, the acting commanding officer. "Go to battle stations!"

Before the crew could respond, a pyronite blast of sufficient proportions to penetrate the ship's repellite hull knocked out everyone aboard. The Maraudians and their three hostages had barely revived by the time they were being boarded. Still unable to move about, the stricken crew could only watch as the metallic soldiers of the Empire attached a bizarre harness of cables to the main control panel and reconfigured the *Maraudor's* instrumentation to accept the tractor beam that the robots would use to tow the space pirates' ship back to Ulantia.

All of this was accomplished without a word as the intruders made everything ready. To confirm their understanding of the Maraudians' exact situation, they used the same mind-scanning device that Terran had used on the Earthlings. After applying the Hat to Mazor and three of the bridge personnel, the robots had the big picture.

Speaking for the first time since their arrival, the head centurion announced, "This entire crew is under arrest for crimes against the Empire. You will all be returned to the Qwarzarian Galaxy and imprisoned on Ulantia."

The crew could do nothing but listen as the mechanical monotoned edict proclaimed that their lives as Pirates of Marauda had come to an end.

Rosario and Knox were in Bob's compartment when the *Maraudor* was boarded. The three had no idea what had just occurred, only that the hatch had rolled shut and they were now confined to quarters.

In the saucer, Terran and his men were feeling nauseous and dizzy as their minds opened to a surge of realizations. There were long moments of silence while new revelations penetrated their understanding like water in a dry sponge. They were struck with the epiphany that they had been looking at their mission in a way that was not only terribly limited, but also grossly inappropriate. What they had perceived as stark differences between themselves and the Earthlings became superficial and inconsequential, and they felt only kinship. Feelings of love, compassion, and fair play were demanding an audience with a sense of conscience they had all but forgotten.

"Hold everything!" said Terran. "The way we are going about this is all wrong. Lieutenant Zane, bring the Earthlings who man this station to me. We must make things right with them. I see now that we can no longer treat people whis way."

"At once, Captain," said Zane as he turned and left the saucer.

"We don't need to plunder and scheme our way through life," Terran continued. "Why, we're only stealing what is freely available to us all! And these Earthlings are not our foes, they're our brothers, as are all humans everywhere."

Zalcon, Mandoon, and the rest of the crew listened attentively to their captain's words—ideas they never expected to hear from the terrible Terran. And yet, as he spoke, they could only agree with him. Their previous ambition to acquire the prize for its untold wealth and power vanished in the presence of the Esseen crystals. The deception was over, as if some terrible joke that had been played on them dissolved with its discovery.

"I remember Rosario and Knox now!" Eli said, gripping his brother's shoulder. "It's the crystals!"

Zoe nodded. "Yes, it's all coming back to me, too…, the storm, the island, the pirates…, and the monsters." He went pale as the memories of their ordeal flooded his mind. "I remember when Dad was killed by those lions..., and finding the Wizard's Hat, Adama, Shakti, and her mother. Man, it's like it all just happened last summer!"

"I realize now," Terran said, looking at the brothers, "that Rosario, Knox, your father, and both of you were instrumental in helping us to reach this remarkable attainment. Commander Mandoon, you will return immediately to the *Maraudor* and retrieve the three Earthlings so they can take part in this experience."

"Yes, Captain," said Mandoon. "Don't forget that there will be a time lapse..., maybe as much as seven days by the time I return."

"Understood," said Terran. "Be that as it may, I think it best to leave the ship where it is for now. Be on your way, sir."

"At once, Captain," Mandoon said, taking his leave just as Zane and Zalcon reentered the saucer with Walsh and his crew following behind.

"Commander Zalcon," said Terran, "you and Lieutenant Zane will conduct a full inspection of this craft and report back to me."

"Yes, sir," said Zalcon, as he and Zane now headed for the top deck.

Still in shock from the surprise attack, Walsh and his men had barely recovered from being stunned by the Maraudian weapons.

Turning to them, Terran said, "Gentlemen, I must apologize. It is regrettable that we had to meet in such drastic circumstances. However, I now believe we will all benefit from this acquaintance."

Walsh was astonished. "I must admit, sir," he said, "I did not expect to hear such words coming from an invader from outerspace. May I ask what your intentions are, now that we are your prisoners?"

"Try to understand," said Terran, "this craft is a chalice for the crystals, the most treasured objects in the Universe. We came here from another galaxy because we thought they would give us unlimited wealth and power, which we now understand they do, but far beyond the material level. The crystals are the common denominator for all humanity, a race that stretches throughout the Universe. It is the influence of the crystals that we are all experiencing right now."

The old sea dog was awestruck. Terran's explanation caused Walsh's eyes to glaze and his jaw to drop. "What you're telling us," he said, "is almost too much to fathom. But here you are, and you've opened the saucer..., a miracle in itself. We had no idea how to gain access to this wonderful spacecraft. We didn't even know that such crystals existed..., let alone their awesome powers. That's why we've been experiencing this marvelous feeling ever since the saucer was surfaced, and even more so now."

"Captain!" called Zane, returning with Zalcon from their inspection. "Every chamber in this craft is identical."

"On each deck," said Zalcon, "there are tables, couches, and all manner of lavish furnishings. Only the bridge is different.

In addition to the cylindrical luminescent shaft in the center of every deck, there is a central chamber on the bridge where I believe the Esseen Crystals may be housed."

"Very well," said Terran. "Take me to the bridge."

The Illuminosity were relentless. Although it was impossible for the robots to benefit from the powers of the Esseen Crystals, they were driven to possess the ultimate treasure in order to stifle its influence on others, for the crystals would curtail the ambitions of the multitudes who supported their empire.

After securing Terran's ship and crew, the tenacious robots moved the *Maraudor* ahead to the twenty-first century and dispatched a squadron of fighters to intercept Terran's team on the planet. None of the half-dozen ships anchored near the sea dock were equipped for confrontation with an enemy like the Illuminosity. The Empire's fighters came soaring in with no regard for the possibility of retaliation, simultaneously attacking the sea dock and the smattering of ships with their sonic weapons.

Then the robot squadron landed, one on each of the four helipads on the sea dock. Clanking in unison, eight robots made their way to the shelter's interior. Finding the time ship's hatch open, they proceeded to the bridge to secure the Esseen Crystals from the central chamber. As Terran and the others lay there, fully conscious but unable to move, the robots went about their business, collecting the two-foot-long crystals from their receptacle and placing them in three repellite chests. Next they searched for the controls of the ship, but could only find a three-foot-diameter transparent sphere fixed to the center of the deck. On either side of the sphere were two metal armchairs. It quickly became obvious that, despite their vast collection of intelligence, they did not have a clue about how to operate a Lamorian time ship. Assuming that the saucer was no longer functional, they soon gave up the idea of making it fly.

Turning to face Terran, the head centurion announced, "Your ship and your crew have been seized. We will take them back to Ulantia with us. You and your officers are to be marooned on this planet as punishment for your crimes against the Empire."

Hearing the robots' intentions, Eli and Zoe were filled with despair. All they could do was picture their father's grim smile and their last promise to return for him.

Without another word, the robots turned and left their victims still paralyzed and lying about.

Although Walsh's SOS had been heard by several of the international participants of the original recovery effort, the first one to respond was a French carrier two hundred miles away. The French immediately sent out eight interceptors, but were unable to establish any further radio contact with the sea dock, leading them to anticipate the worst.

As the four falconesque fighters of the Illuminosity began their vertical ascent from the helipads of the sea dock, the French interceptors came streaking by, executing a sharp banking turn that aligned them with their targets, which were now only fifty feet above the surface. The French pilots had no way of knowing that these were the sea dock's second set of alien visitors since receiving Walsh's SOS.

"*Zut alors!* I don' recognize zem," shouted the lead plane's wingman.

Without delay, the squadron leader issued a challenge to the alien birds as they continued to gain altitude: "Identify yourselves or we fire! Zis will be your only warning!"

The flight leader did not expect an answer. Allowing only a split second for a response, he ordered his birds to arm their missiles and fire. Without hesitation, all eight jets unleashed a sixteen air-to-air rocket fusillade. Every missile impacted on its target as the flock of interceptors peeled off and away. The combined explosions sent a tremendous shock wave into the sea dock, causing it to convulse violently in the water.

As the smoke cleared, it became evident that the sea dock, although still intact, was the *only* thing affected by the horrendous barrage as the four alien fighters continued their ascent unscathed. There was no reciprocal exchange, no indication of tactical concern. After their unhindered vertical climb, the four spacecraft accelerated across the sky and out of sight at lightning speed.

When the French fighters returned for another exchange, they found themselves alone in the sky. Unable to track their opponents, they could do little else than circle the sea dock several times and return to their carrier.

Another hour passed before everyone on the sea dock and

the surrounding ships regained their coordination. Within the time ship, the absence of the stolen crystals was soon apparent. Their influence was still present but now somewhat diminished.

Walsh was frantic. "I can't believe," he said, "that we weren't all killed by those things. What are they…, robots?"

"Exactly," Terran replied. "Robots of the Illuminosity Empire. Our survival is no surprise. The robots rarely exterminate any intelligent beings. In fact, I'm sure they intend to return at some point, now that they are aware of this galaxy and your world. They will no doubt seek to include you, too, in their empire."

Walsh and the sea dock crew were aghast.

"Why?" asked Walsh. "What could our world possibly have to offer to make them come so far?"

"Their main objective," Terran explained, "is to harvest intelligence for its own sake. They pursue this objective relentlessly. It is the primary directive of the algorithm that governs their existence."

"You mean," said Walsh, "that they farm humans like cattle…, and instead of meat, intelligence is what they're after?"

"Yes, that's precisely what I'm telling you. The robot empire is known as the Illuminosity. They outlived the race that created them eons ago. The entire human population of their home planet, Ulantia, is comprised of prisoners from other worlds, enslaved for crimes against the empire. The Illuminosity rule all of the three known populated galaxies…, or I should say, *four*, now that they have discovered *your* presence. They control their vast herds of humanity through consumer incentives of wealth and power, stimulated by an endless stream of gadgets and games, together with an inclusive propaganda whose ultimate effect is to hypnotize and fascinate."

As Terran spoke, he began to realize the bigger picture.

All this time, the joke has been on us. We never had a chance. Right from the start, the robots knew everything we did..., everything we said. Every heist, the time portal, the Hat, the scanners, and all the other technology we have stolen was actually made available to us while our every action was monitored and recorded. We were always doing their bidding. We were always just one of their controlled experiments..., pawns of a mindless, all-powerful empire. I see it so clearly now. It was our greed, which they constantly stimulated, that kept us blind and unaware. I can see why they confiscated the Esseen Crystals. It is the power of the crystals that has opened my eyes.

When the sky barge burst back into the past, circling the sapphire Earth within the orbit of its silver moon, the space wizard could not believe his eyes. The *Maraudor* was gone! Unless the time portal were programmed otherwise, he knew it was impossible to arrive back anywhere else but the exact point of departure.

"How can this be?" he shrieked.

But there was no answer to his rhetorical question from his three-man crew, for they, too, were stunned at the absence of their mother ship.

"What can it mean?" asked the helmsman.

"Chief Mazor would never maroon us here!" said the co-pilot.

"What could have made him leave without us?" demanded the engineer.

And then, in an instant, as if an announcement had been made, they all realized what had happened.

"The robots!" cried the helmsman. "They found us! That must be it."

"Of course!" said Mandoon. "The Empire tracked us by our trail of time spikes. It's the only answer. I *told* Terran this could happen."

Mandoon's heart sank as he realized that the adventurous life they loved was over. He immediately set a course for the sea dock.

"We must get back to the captain as quickly as possible!" he said.

The helmsman responded, "Course is laid in, and we're ready to go, sir!"

"Make it so!"

"What about the time differential, Captain?" the helmsman asked.

"There's nothing we can do about that. I only hope they're still there when we arrive."

As soon as the robots extracted the crystals from the saucer, their miraculous effects became conspicuously absent from the populations of Earth, causing them to rapidly regress into their former state of turmoil and calamity. Gone were the radiating emanations of benevolence that had given the peoples of the planet their hope, inspiration, and enchantment. This global cerebral crash manifested in a sea of pandemonium as crime and negativity broke out all over like a blistering rash. Brotherly love and selflessness were replaced once again with greed, selfishness, and fear.

The tyrannical governments of the world, which had been at the brink of extinction, seized this moment to reinstate their guise of protection, claiming that the Earth was on the verge of destruction unless everyone returned at once to the edicts of sacrifice and servitude. Overnight, the military and police forces of every nation clamped down on freedoms of movement and speech. The major premise used to justify all this was that the Earth had been attacked by extraterrestrials. Until a sense of security could be reestablished, martial law would be in effect indefinitely. Within a few short days, any remnants of the new philanthropic way of life were extinct.

Only those aboard the sea dock remained as before. Now, after hearing the Maraudians' explanations for their attack, Captain Walsh and all fifteen members of his command were sympathetic to them.

Crestfallen, Eli said to Terran, "We understand now what brought this all about, Captain...., but it doesn't bring our father back."

"There must be *something* we can do," Zoe insisted.

"But we are marooned here," said Terran. "I am afraid all I can do is apologize."

"Captain Terran," said Walsh, "I've been monitoring the reports on global affairs. It seems that the wave of enlightenment that the rest of the world has been experiencing is over. Martial law is now in effect everywhere. My government is calling for the sea dock's elimination. I don't think it will be long before they come here to annihilate us."

"Understood, Captain Walsh," said Terran. "Everyone gather supplies. We will go into the time ship and seal the hatch!"

No sooner had Zoe closed the hatch behind him and the others than Terran's radio came alive with the frantic pitch of a highly agitated Mandoon.

"Captain, the *Maraudor* has vanished! We are returning to your location."

"Yes," Terran said, "the Empire has found us. They took the crystals and seized our ship and crew. We have been marooned here."

The captain's message confirmed Mandoon's worst fears as the sky barge pierced the clouds over the sea dock.

"We'll be landing momentarily, Captain."

As Mandoon spoke, he could see a flurry of air traffic over the landing zone.

"Arm yourselves and prepare to disembark with the time portal as soon as we arrive," Mandoon ordered.

When the sky barge landed on the helipad, the crew hastened to carry out their orders. Mandoon and his men were already running down the ramp with the time portal when Terran's voice came over the ship's speakers.

"Use your weapons if necessary! Hurry, we're waiting to open the hatch for you!"

Moving as fast as they could, Mandoon's team came under fire from a helicopter's blazing 50-caliber machine gun. In the midst of the strafing, with bullets landing only inches away from their feet, Mandoon and his helmsman returned fire with their sonic weapons as the other two crew members, carrying the time portal, scurried down the seventy-five-foot walkway to the sea dock. Both sonic blasts hit the chopper, causing it to veer off and then drop into the ocean.

As the four men scrambled toward the entry to the dock, a second chopper appeared and hurled two rockets into the sky barge, which exploded and fell away into the sea. After taking direct hits from both missiles, the landing pad was completely engulfed in flames. When the chopper came overhead, all but one of the Maraudians had made it through the sea dock entrance—the unfortunate wounded helmsman had been thrown into a watery grave.

Once inside, Mandoon and the other two men collapsed in the saucer as Eli sealed the hatch behind them.

Bob, Rosario, and Knox had slept several times in their sealed compartment since they had been inexplicably stunned.

"How much longer can this go on?" Bob asked. "Judging from my hunger, I'd say it's already been four or five days."

"Aye, sounds about right," Knox agreed. "Why don't those blokes feed us?"

"It *is* strange," Bob said, "when you consider that they could've finished us off any time they wanted to."

"Unless they've decided to starve us to death," said Rosario. "Keeping us here like this would be the easiest way to do the deed."

That speculation seemed reasonable.

Bob hardly noticed Rosario's wide-eyed expression anymore. He couldn't explain the kinship he now felt for this ancient mariner and his first mate.

"Sometimes," Bob said, "it feels like the ship's moving, but I can't say for sure."

"Aye," said Knox, "that thought came to me as well. What do *you* think, Cap'n?"

Rosario thought for a moment. "No way of telling." Then, turning to Bob, he said, "I wonder what became of your sons. Why haven't they returned to us?"

"I'm afraid," said Bob, "something terrible may have happened. I hate to think of what it could be, but this sudden isolation is a drastic change from the way we *were* being treated. Whatever it is, it adds up to bad news for my boys and for us. Locked away like this, we have no chance at all. It's only a matter of time now. Let's face it…, we can't last much longer. It sure is a lousy way to go."

"If we're to be done away with," said Knox, "I would 'ave preferred a quick slit across the throat."

"It doesn't make sense," Rosario said. "We still have water. If they mean to do away with us, why don't they cut *that* off?"

The conversation dwindled into silence and somber contemplation as the three hostages could do nothing but endure another cycle of sleep and starvation. Not wanting to add any more misery to the mood, Bob silently wondered how many more cycles like this it would take to end it all.

"What now, Captain?" Mandoon said, trying to catch his breath. He was standing by what was left of his away team as they set the time portal down.

Before Terran could answer, Eli jumped up and said, "What *now?!* It's obvious. We can't give up! We've gotta go after the robots and rescue our dad…. And get back your ship, Captain, and those crystals. I know we can come up with *some*thing. Come on, now! Time's a wasting!"

"I understand your desperation," Terran said consolingly, "but I am afraid there is nothing we can do. It seems we are truly marooned here. Our sky barge has been destroyed. But even if it were still intact, we could never chase the Illuminosity across the galaxies with it. Besides, if we *were* able to pursue the robots, we would be ill advised to do so. They are formidable opponents, to say the least. The robots and their ships are made of repellite, the most durable substance in the Universe. This, together with their perpetual algorithmic technology, makes them indestructible."

"We've *gotta* come up with a better answer than that," Eli insisted. "We're *not* giving up! There *must* be some way out of this."

Terran shook his head. "If anyone has any ideas, I am ready to hear them."

"Captain," said Zalcon excitedly, "we still have the time portal. Why can't we use it to go back to when we still had the *Maraudor?*"

"Of course!" said Terran. "That's so obvious! Mandoon, make it so!"

The space wizard frowned. "I'm afraid, Captain, that would only make our situation worse. The robots know everything about us, and can easily chase us anywhere in space and time. Then we would *all* be their prisoners. At least, now that is not the case."

"You're right, Mandoon. At least, this way we are safely sealed within the time ship."

"But there might be another way," said Mandoon, stroking his straggly beard. "This time ship would have no trouble pursuing the robots if we could only master its controls."

"Yeah," Eli said. "We got in *here*, didn't we? Let's see what else we can do."

Zoe looked at his brother. "Man," he said, "we're talking

about space travel here!"

"Whatever it takes!" Eli shot back. "We can't just give up if there's any chance at all."

Terran looked at Mandoon skeptically. "Master the ship's controls, Commander?" he said. "If you haven't noticed, there seems to be a distinct *absence* of controls on this bridge. Even the robots could not find a way to activate this craft. That shows what we're up against."

But Mandoon wasn't listening. He was busy examining the two metal armchairs in the center of the bridge that were distinctly different from any of the other furnishings on the ship.

"Captain Terran, sir," said Walsh, "I've been monitoring the media news on my laptop and I believe you should be aware of what's going on out there."

"What is it, Mister Walsh?"

"Since your attack on the sea dock, everyone believes that the Earth has been invaded by aliens. People are unaware that the subsequent attack by the robots was from a separate force. They believe that you and the robots are one and the same, and that you have done something to the saucer that has terminated the effects they had been experiencing. The world is in a state of panic and it's getting worse every minute. The American government, as well as that of every other nation, has seized this opportunity to invoke martial law and curtail general freedoms. As I speak, the annihilation of the sea dock and everything in its perimeter is imminent. I would guess that the attack will come within the next forty-eight hours..., if not minutes."

"What I don't understand," Terran said, "is how come the rest of world no longer feels the effects of the crystals, and we still do."

"What if...?" Mandoon said, pointing to the cylindrical chamber in the center of the bridge, "what if some of the crystals are still aboard?"

Terran's eyebrows rose at this. "I cannot think of any other explanation," he said. "It would make sense that the time ship would have its own power supply..., perhaps even a perpetual power source. We should be safe as long as we stay within this craft. No amount of Earthly destruction can penetrate our repellite hull."

"Be that as it may, sir," Mandoon said, "unless we can activate this craft, I am afraid that all we will have is an impregnable tomb beneath the sea."

"Captain," Walsh said, "may I have your permission to see my men off in the lifeboats? I myself, however, would like to remain with you to see this thing through."

"Permission granted," said Terran. "Get them away immediately before it's too late."

"Aye, Captain. I'll have to alert the authorities that my men are leaving and request a sea rescue."

"But Captain Walsh," pleaded his radioman, Chief Briggs, "we don't want to leave you here! Please come with us."

The rest of Walsh's crew concurred.

"Yes, Captain, this is not our problem. Your place is with us."

"Please, sir. It's your only chance."

Walsh put up his hands. "Men, I've had a long and adventurous career. I'm not ready for the mothball fleet yet, and leaving with you all would pretty much ensure my retirement. I believe I can still be of some service if I stay aboard. I've decided to continue on with Captain Terran's crew to wherever that may lead."

"You have been most helpful to us, Captain Walsh," Terran said. "It will be an honor to have you along."

This state of grace and elegance, which was now the space pirate's demeanor, went unquestioned by his crew, though not unnoticed. Zalcon, Zane, and Mandoon agreed with their captain in silent acknowledgment.

"Captain Terran," said Walsh, "I'll have to go to the sea dock's radio room to call the Coast Guard."

"Agreed."

Walsh gathered his men. "There are two survival boats," he told them. "You can start for Bermuda, and the rescue teams will meet you along the way. I'm sure you won't have long to wait before they arrive. Our supplies were due to be replenished when this whole thing started, and now they're almost exhausted. Take only a minimal amount of food and water with you. The supplies here are limited."

As Walsh and his crew started toward the hatch, Eli held up his hand. "You'll need *this*," he said, inserting his hand into the indentation, which caused the hatch to open.

"Get back as soon as you can," Terran called after Walsh. "I don't know how long we can leave the hatch open."

Watching Eli open the hatch, Mandoon got an idea. Walking over to the transparent sphere in the center of the bridge, he sat down in one of the two metal armchairs. Placing his hands on the armrests, he realized that there was more to these chairs than he had previously noticed. On each outside rail, there was a round button. However, when he pressed them, they wouldn't move.

Mandoon spun around to face Eli. "Come over here and sit down," he said, pointing to the other chair. "Let's see what happens."

As Eli sat in the chair, he looked at Mandoon and shrugged. "Nothing's happening," he said.

Mandoon's eyes were ablaze with anticipation. "Now feel those buttons on each side of the armrest.... Press on them."

When Eli did this, two indented hand pods from underneath the armrests snapped up into position.

"Aha!" Mandoon exclaimed. "Captain, come and see what we have found!"

Two more timeless cycles of sleep and starvation had the three hostages feeling weak and severely depressed. Their conversations had dwindled to a few words from time to time as they entered this extreme phase of their internment.

Bob's only thoughts now were about his sons. He wondered if they were still alive and if he would ever see them again. Gone was his usual optimism. Now he was all but convinced that his boys were dead.

Otherwise, they would have made their way back to me by now.

Even though starvation seemed inevitable, his only thought was the fate of his sons.

Like the Earthlings, Terran's crew on the *Maraudor* had been confined to their quarters with nothing but water ever since the robots had seized their ship. Now, as the metallic jailors made their second maintenance visit, they finally released the Maraudians to relieve their hunger.

Looking around, Chief Mazor was the first to realize that the robots had overlooked something.

"There are three others still locked in their quarters," he said. "You had better release them as well, or they'll be dead before much longer."

One of the robots pressed a button on a control panel. "Go see to their needs," it said.

Suddenly, Bob, Rosario, and Knox heard the familiar clank of the hatch rolling open. There, staring in at them and smiling grimly, were four Maraudian crew members. That the Earthlings did not know the Maraudians' names did not diminish their appreciation as they staggered to their feet and stepped out into the passageway. They were weak and unsteady, but their will to carry on had been rekindled.

"Sorry we took so long," said Chief Mazor. "They have the ship rigged so we cannot operate."

"What's 'appened?" asked Knox. "*Who's* got the ship rigged?"

"Let us get you some food," said the chief, "and then we'll tell you all about it."

By the time Bob, Rosario, and Knox scarfed down a second plate of space vittles, the crew had brought the three Earthlings up to date.

"We were all confined to quarters," said one of the six-foot space pirates, "until they figured out that we would all be dead if they did not let us out and about."

"It took a little longer to release you," said Mazor, "because they did not know you were aboard until I told them."

Bob's first reaction to what he was hearing was that his sons were probably alive, and there might still be a chance they could somehow all be together again. But his elation was short-lived as he came to understand that they were all prisoners of the Illuminosity and on their way back to the Qwarzarian Galaxy. After considering this current chain of events, Bob realized that he would have to put aside his bitterness for the space pirates.

Exiled to another galaxy…. That's it, then…, done for. Anyway, it's not these space pirates' fault. Afterall, they're just treasure hunters like the rest of us. Nobody to blame but myself. It was our own discovery of that saucer that brought about this whole mess. I'll never see my boys again. My life might as well be over. All I can hope for now is a chance to destroy these robots.

No sooner had Eli placed his hand into the indentation than the central chamber lit up. Golden particles within the transparent column illuminated the whole interior of the bridge.

Suddenly, the sphere between the two command chairs came alive with an amber gaseous cloud, which transformed into the beautiful face of a young woman.

"I see you, Elias," she said, opening her eyes and gazing directly at Eli. "You only have to speak, and I will make it so."

Everyone stood dumbfounded, trying to fathom what was happening.

"I..., I don't understand what you're telling me," Eli said.

"I am the Lamorian vessel, Veda. You may command me, and I shall respond."

"Are you saying," Mandoon asked, "that we can take off and travel through space?"

Veda looked at Mandoon but remained silent. As her eyes penetrated the space wizard's, he was astonished.

She's not a projected image..., she's a living being..., the soul of a living spacecraft!

Zoe was on the same track. "My God!" he said. "This is like a chapter out of the *Arabian Nights*. This craft is *alive*, and *she's* the genie of the lamp!" Jumping into the second command chair and placing his hand in the indentation as Eli had done, he asked her, "Can you fly this ship?"

"I see you, Zoroaster," Veda said, turning toward him. "I am a living craft, and my mind's eye is this sphere. It is within my power to take you anywhere in space or time."

When Zoe heard this extraordinary promise, he was elated.

"Then, you can take us to the Qwarzarian Galaxy, so we can rescue Dad!"

"We can travel to Qwarz, or anywhere else you may desire," said the genie, smiling.

Terran also smiled at this turn of events.

"Zoe," he said, "ask her if we can overtake the robots before they get back to Ulantia."

When Zoe repeated Terran's question, Veda responded, "Indeed, we can and will, if you so desire."

"Eli," Zalcon said, "ask her about supplies. How will we be able to sustain ourselves on such a long journey?"

To Eli's question, the genie responded, "Your desires are all that is necessary."

"I can see no reason," said Terran, "not to take Veda's word for everything she says."

At that moment, looking highly excited, Walsh came running in from seeing his men off in the lifeboats. "We can expect a massive attack on this sea dock within the hour!" he announced.

Terran immediately responded, "Make ready for departure!"

But, aside from the two pilots in the command chairs and the genie in the sphere, there were no stations to be manned.

"Captain," said Zalcon, "what about the roof of the sea dock? Are we going to blast right through it?"

Terran paused a moment to think.

"I'll go back to the control room," said Walsh, "and release the pins that will allow the dock to separate into two sections.

That will clear us for takeoff."

"Make it so, Mr. Walsh," said Terran, "and get back aboard as quickly as you can."

"Aye, Sir," Walsh said, and was off to do the deed.

These were trying times for the peoples of Earth. The great benevolence that had permeated every aspect of life on the planet with the promise of everlasting peace and well being now seemed like a distant dream. It was the morning after, and the world had a dreadful hangover. The miraculous effects of the Esseen Crystals had quickly dwindled, leaving the quality of life worse than ever.

In America, President Ivy had reclaimed his merciless grip on the masses by the only means he knew—fear. Vox News relentlessly fanned the fires of despair with stories of the devastation the alien invasion would cast over humanity. Although Ivy never knew that it was the crystals that had nearly dismantled the engines of his avarice, he believed that the phenomenon originated with the alien craft, and was therefore determined to annihilate the sea dock and everything in it.

Separating the sea dock into two sections was not as simple as Walsh had thought. There were several steps to the procedure that he was not familiar with. The needed information from various manuals and classified documents took as much time to locate as to implement. All during that time, Walsh kept his laptop tuned to the constant flow of blather about the dire threat that the sea dock posed to the world.

"We will use four blockbusters to take out the target," said General Colin of the U.S. Air Force. "I doubt there will be anything left to identify after that."

"It certainly *sounds* like that will do the job," said a reporter. "But tell us, General, what if it doesn't?"

"We are prepared to follow up with nuclear weapons, if necessary. As I speak, the first wave of bombers is on its way."

As soon as Walsh had the massive locking pins disengaged, the two sections began to separate—but faster than he had anticipated, as the moderate chop rocked the sections apart. Seeing this, the old sub commander raced from the second-floor control room down the stairs and toward the open hatch of the saucer. The sound of approaching aircraft urged him on. But he could see that the span between the dock and the hatch was already too great to make the leap.

Waiting by the hatch, Zalcon and two of his men immediately realized Walsh's predicament.

Zalcon called back to the bridge, "We're drifting too far from the dock. We must close the distance, or Walsh will never make it."

Placing his hand on Eli's shoulder, Terran told him to make it so.

"Veda," Eli said, "take us back toward the dock. We have a man to rescue."

As soon as Eli uttered the words, the saucer began to close the distance.

But then four jets came streaking in and let their blockbusters go. Hearing their whistles, Walsh leaped across the water into Zalcon's waiting arms. The two tumbled backward into the craft as the hatch closed without a second to spare.

The four 8,000-pounders slammed into the sea dock, causing a horrendous eruption of fire and torn steel. What had been a symbolic monument to the coexistence of all the peoples of the world was no more. When the smoke finally cleared, all that remained of the target was the saucer floating unscathed in the troubled waters.

Inside the Lamorian time ship, the crew were unaware that the sea dock had been obliterated. All they experienced was a moderate jolt and a dull roar.

When a single F-22 came by to assess the damage, the pilot could hardly control his amazement as he reported what he saw. "My God!" he exclaimed. "It's still there! The sea dock was destroyed, but the saucer is just floating there like nothing's happened. I repeat..., the main target is unscathed. We're gonna need more than four blockbusters for this baby. Colonel Thomson..., returning to base."

Minutes after Thomson made his report, a second wave of jets came in and hurled a dozen missiles into the obstinate target.

Again, within the marvelous craft, the crew experienced

only a series of muffled thuds on the bulkhead.

Zoe paid little attention to the sounds and vibrations caused by the turmoil outside.

"What's the plan, Captain?" he said. "We want our father back, and I assume you feel the same way about your ship and crew. Time's a wasting, and the Illuminosity is getting away."

Terran did not have all the answers, but he was clear about what was next.

"You and your brother," he said, "must pilot this craft, and my officers and I will determine our strategy. How we will deal with the robots when and if we catch up to them remains to be seen. Everyone, take a seat! We're getting under way!"

Everyone sat down and hung on to their seats.

"Zoe," Terran ordered, "ask Veda to take us away from this place and into orbit while we figure out how to pinpoint our destination."

Looking directly into the genie's eyes, Zoe said, "Veda, please do as Captain Terran has asked."

The saucer immediately lifted off, ascending through the hellfire hurled at it by the Earthlings.

Moments later, Veda smiled. "It is done," she said. As she spoke, her image dissolved into a view of the saucer in orbit around the troubled planet below.

"Captain," Mandoon said, "I suggest we use the time portal to return to the temporal corridor where we last left the *Marau-dor*. It was the Earth year 1890. Perhaps we can pick up their trail if we start from that point in time."

Nodding, Terran said, "Eli, tell Veda our plan."

But before Eli could respond, the genie said, "In reality, there is only now. All you need to do to navigate me is indicate exactly *what* you are looking for."

As she spoke, the image of the saucer dissolved into a pulsating hologram of the Universe. Everyone gathered around the sphere, riveted to what was unfolding.

"What you see before you," the enthralling voice explained, "is known as the cosmic day and the cosmic night. Each cycle of creation, as it expands and collapses over immeasurable time, is the cosmic moment known as now. You have only to indicate a point in time and space, and I will take you there."

The whole ship's company stood speechless as they tried to fathom Veda's flawless eloquence and their own new capabilities.

"Can we plot a course to intercept the Illuminosity?" Eli asked.

"There is no place they can go," she responded, "that we cannot follow."

Terran laid his hand on Eli's shoulder and said, "Make it so."

Now that the men of the *Maraudor* had freedom to move about the ship, they found their dire situation a little more tolerable. That they were all prisoners of the Illuminosity served to bond the Earthlings and the remainer of Terran's crew. But, so far, even their combined efforts had failed to produce any kind of plan that would allow them to turn the tables on the robots.

"These star cruisers are capable of fantastic speeds," Chief Mazor explained. "But even at top speed, the trip back to Ulantia will be long and monotonous. And that will only be the beginning of our new life of slavery…, unless we can come up with an effective plan to take over the ship."

"I don't know, Chief," said Bob. "So far, everything we've thought of has failed. It didn't work when we tried to disconnect the robots' harness on the primary control panel, and we couldn't activate the ship's self-destruct sequence, either."

"Right," said one of the Maraudians. "It was the robots who designed and built the *Maraudor*, so it's no surprise that they can rig the ship like this."

"Yes," said Mazor, "just the fact that they let us move about and meet and talk like this in the mess hall shows they have little concern about our ability to resist."

As time passed with no spark of hope, everyone sank into a deep depression.

Periodically, using one of the *Maraudor's* sky barges, a small contingent of robots came aboard to ensure that the ship's controls were still paralyzed. Mazor and his men were always present on the bridge during these visits, watching and waiting for any sign of weakness that they might use for their advantage. However, the robots conducted their business in silence, never acknowledging their prisoners in any way. The crew's attempts to communicate with their captors were ignored, if they were heard at all.

The chief discovered this early on when he walked up to one of the robots and said in a loud, clear voice, "I would like to speak to your captain."

After repeating his request three times, he turned and went back to his men.

"No harm in trying," he said, sitting down on the deck.

The whole experience of being controlled and ignored cast a grim picture of what they could expect internment might be like when they reached Ulantia.

Waking from another of countless sleep cycles, Bob realized that he had reached the bottom of the bottom. Something within liberated him to accept the fact that his doom was sealed. His thoughts of never again seeing his sons melded with memories of philosophical discussions they had often had together.

"One thing's for sure," Eli had once said, "we have this life right now, and I'm gonna make the most of it."

"That's right, bro," Zoe had said. "Life is short."

"Well," Bob had said, "I've come to believe that life is eternal, and each lifetime, in reality, is another day in that eternal life. Each of those days is precious and not to be squandered. But sometimes such extreme circumstances arise that suicide can become the logical course."

Now it seemed that just such a dire situation was at hand. If so, Bob would take heart in selling his life at as dear a price as he could exact from the robots.

Mazor was still in his bunk when Bob burst into the compartment to infuse the chief with his newfound enthusiasm.

"No matter what the cost," Bob said, "we've gotta find some way to make them pay, some way to destroy them or eject them out into space!"

While the humans aboard the *Maraudor* schemed and planned as best they could, the robots modified their intentions as well. Just before leaving the Milky Way Galaxy, the Illuminosity changed course to head for the constellation Sagittarius, where the nearest black hole was located. Although this change of course would be a considerable addition to the extreme distance they had yet to cross before reaching the Qwarzarian Galaxy, the robots planned to deposit the Esseen Crystals in a place where they would remain forever lost to the vast populations of their empire. The miraculous powers afforded by the Esseen Crystals had no place in their grand scheme. The crystals could only undermine the incentives already in place to stimulate the humans' consumerism.

As yet, Terran and his new crew still had much to discover about Veda's full capabilities and their own potential. Streaking through the cosmos to overtake their quarry seemed pointless, given that once they caught up to the invincibles, they had no viable means of overpowering them.

Terran stood by Eli and Zoe as they sat in their command chairs on either side of the all-knowing sphere.

"Well," he said, "we know that we can overtake the space devils. What we don't know is how we are going to deal with them."

"Yes, Captain," said Zalcon, "no doubt the crystals are aboard the mother ship. We'll need to gain entry somehow. And then, of course, there are the men and the *Maraudor* itself to consider."

"What weapons does this craft possess?" asked Zane. "We'll need more than sonic cannons to take on those repellite-hulled robots. The fact that they successfully seized the *Maraudor* speaks of superior weaponry. They must have used pyronite or some secret device that can penetrate repellite."

"Even if we had pyronite torpedoes," Zalcon said, "we would run the risk of destroying the ship and losing the crystals."

"That's right," said Zane, "but since we don't have any pyronite, it's a moot point."

With a twinkle in his eye, Walsh chimed in, "Didn't you say the robots are driven by an algorithm?"

"What are you driving at, Mister Walsh?" Terran asked.

"Well," Walsh said with a grin, "I've had some experience with torpedoes that used algorithms to cause robots to malfunction. Perhaps this can be done to these robots as well."

A smile started to curl the corners of Terran's mouth.

A seed for a plan!

"You may have something there," said Mandoon. "Yes…, if we could come up with the right frequency, it just might be that simple. We could neutralize them with a contrary algorithm."

With new fire in his eyes, Terran asked, "How could we concoct such a weapon? There is no machinery or tools on board. Every compartment contains only furniture."

"I'm sure Veda can help us with these problems," Zoe said. "She's gotten us this far."

Nodding to Zoe, Terran said, "Give it a try."

As Zoe started to explain the situation to the sphere, Veda's image replaced that of the Universe.

"The machines you have described," she said, "were created by humans. We are capable of neutralizing them. Your desire to do so is all that is required."

Everyone fell silent. The genie's reply was almost too simple to be believed.

Terran's mind raced ahead.

If all that is required is desire, then our problems are over.

"It sounds like we can do this if we can catch them," he said. "Can she show us where they are now?"

As Eli turned toward the sphere, Veda's image dissolved back into a model of the sea of space and time, which expanded and collapsed in intervals. The pulsating image froze in its expanded phase.

"We are *here*," said Veda's voice. As she said this, a red twinkling light indicated the saucer's position. "The machines are *there*." A similar green light appeared, showing the Illuminosity's position.

How can such a thing be possible? Terran wondered.

"How are you able to pinpoint the crystals so easily?" he

asked, looking directly at the sphere.

But before Eli could put the question to the genie, she reappeared.

"No matter where the crystals are," she explained, looking directly at Terran, "they are as one with the *One called Me*. Their location could never be a mystery to me, for we are one."

After reflecting for a moment, Terran said, "When I studied the sacred hieroglyphs on Qwarz, I learned that the Esseen Crystals belong to the cradle race. I have heard the legends of their amazing powers, and I have experienced firsthand their ability to guide man along the path of enlightenment. We know the robots took the crystals, but I can feel the influence even now. Are there still crystals aboard this ship?"

Again, looking directly into the captain's eyes, Veda answered, "It is true that the precious crystals within the central chamber are missing. However, this ship is alive with its own crystals, which can never be removed. This ship is the chalice, the Middle of the Middle. Here the influences of the divine Esseen Crystals are always present."

Terran was listening in amazement.

That means Mandoon's theory was correct. We have actually achieved every Maraudian's lifelong dream. We've found the Esseen Crystals! According to the legend, we are now in the presence of the ultimate power of the Universe!

After a long pause, he simply said, "I understand."

The failure of the prisoners aboard the *Maraudor* to hinder their captors in any way left them feeling helpless and demoralized. After repeated attempts, Chief Mazor still could not disengage the apparatus on the bridge that connected the ship to the robots' tractor beam.

"As long as the beam is on," he said, "there's no way to access the controls. Even if we could take back command of the bridge, that still wouldn't solve the larger problem. We need a plan that will eliminate the machines, or at least lessen their numbers."

"Agreed," said Bob. "There's gotta be some way to get to them. We have to find it. We must make them pay as high a price as possible."

"I was thinking," said Mazor, "the robots come back every couple of sleep cycles to check their equipment. They would have to shut down the tractor beam whenever they land or leave."

"If that's the case, we won't have much time to make our move."

At that, Knox jumped to his feet. "What if we 'id in one o' those sky barges?" he said. "When the beam, or whatever it is, goes off, we could make our escape."

"Yes," Mazor said, "that would be one way to go. Even though the sky barge won't sustain us long in deep space, at least we could go out fighting. We could use the pyronite torpedoes and maybe take the robots out with us."

They realized that they had come face to face with a plan that, if successful, would ensure their own extinction.

Bob smiled. "Now we're getting somewhere. At least, we can see a fissure in their technology. Maybe somehow we can crack it wide open!"

"Well," said the chief, "we don't feel when they disengage the beam in order to dock..., only when they turn it back on. That's when we feel it taking hold of the ship. Now that I think of it, I can't remember feeling the beam ever turn on when the robots are here..., only after they've left. That would mean they leave the beam off the whole time, relying on inertia for the two ships to stay on course."

"We need to know how long the beam is actually down each time," Bob said. "Then, when we come up with a plan of action, we'll know how long we have to get it done."

"They been comin' every couple o' sleeps like clockwork," said Knox. "That means they'll be 'ere soon. All we 'ave to do is keep a watch and time their visit."

Mazor smiled. "Leave that to me," he said.

Terran was no longer a space pirate caught up in the promise of plunder. The phenomenal influence of the crystals, personified with Veda's eloquence, had transformed him.

While the Lamorian time ship streaked across the galaxy in pursuit of the robots, Eli and Zoe sat in their command chairs, and the rest of the crew focused on the genie. The questions continued to flow from the captain as he stood before the sphere.

"You say we have the ability to defeat them in battle if we desire to do so. How is that possible?"

"You possess within you," Veda responded, "the ability to provide all things in abundance. Their defeat is a matter of belief. You must see their undoing in your mind's eye. As you believe, so shall you manifest."

Still not grasping what he was hearing, Terran accepted Veda's answer at face value. The bridge remained silent as he continued, "How long until we can overtake the robots?"

"It is a considerable distance from here to the Qwarzarian Galaxy," Veda told them. "However, there is still time to intercept the metallics before they reach the abyss at the edge of this galaxy."

Everyone shuddered at the word *abyss*. Zoe and Eli looked at each other, not wanting to believe what they were hearing.

"Veda," Terran said, "please show us the star charts again."

The image of the section of the galaxy they were heading for at an unimaginable speed appeared, confirming their direst apprehensions. Despite the brothers' inexperience, they had no trouble recognizing that what Veda was calling the abyss was, in fact, the Sagittarian Complex.

"Why are they going *there*?" Zoe asked the genie. "It's a black hole!"

"The robots have no use for the sacred crystals. If the human populations they control ever came in contact with the crystals, the Illuminosity's empire would crumble. It seems logical that they intend to cast your ship, along with the crystals, into the abyss before continuing on to Ulantia."

The centurions landed the sky barge right on schedule. As they clanked through the hangar deck hatchway, Chief Mazor was waiting, concealed in an equipment locker directly across from the entryway. Feeling the slight thud as the barge connected with the docking collar, he knew that this indicated the tractor beam was now disengaged. Even before the robots came through the hatch, Mazor started his timing device.

Regardless of which plan the prisoners devised, timing would be essential. Ironically, their plan to go out fighting had rekindled their hope to survive their ordeal, so they decided to save the sky barge plan as a last resort. But for now, they would continue to try to find some way to sabotage their captors.

It was not abnormal for the crew members to be on the bridge as the robots performed their tasks, except that this time the hostages scrutinized every move the robots made as they checked and adjusted the strange mechanism they had attached to the central controls of the *Maraudor*. The would-be saboteurs did not recognize anything in these procedures that they could use to penetrate, probe, or adjust the controls.

Bob and Rosario were also present, watching the robots' every move.

"Well," Rosario whispered as the robots started back for the hangar deck, "if these contraptions operate the same way next time, which they always appear to do, it seems we have less than an hour to execute our plan."

"A little more than half an hour," Bob said. "I can hold my breath for three minutes, and I've done that twelve times since they came aboard."

"Yes," said Rosario, "that could be either all the time we need..., or not nearly enough. We have no way of knowing. I doubt we would know how to foul their rigging, even if there *is* such a thing."

"Foul their rigging?" Bob said. "Yes, foul their rigging! That may be it! We could snare them somehow. Maybe we could throw a heavy net over them or wrap them up in a heavy blanket. Get them so entangled they wouldn't be able to get free, while we push them through the hatch, out into space." Bob was grasping at any fragment of an idea. "Besides," he said, "if that doesn't work, there's always the space barge."

As the robots clanked their way through the hangar deck and back aboard their shuttlecraft, Mazor watched every move they made. Just after the sky barge departed, he could feel the slight tremor of the tractor beam reengaging. The two star cruisers now resumed their journey to their dark destination.

On the bridge of the *Maraudor*, all of the prisoners assembled to compare their sparse observations. Before proceeding, however, Mazor activated the ship's collision alarm. Untouched by the paralyzing effect of the robots' apparatus, the alarm blazed out its message of distress.

"The walls have ears," Mazor explained. "This will jam their attempts to hear our plans…. I precisely timed their procedure at thirty-seven minutes and twelve seconds…, but I could detect no potential for sabotage. Any thoughts about what we can do?"

Bob stepped forward. "Captain Rosario has a scheme…, foul their rigging."

"That's it, Cap'n!" said Knox. "You know, like the traps they used to snare monkeys in the islands…, with a noose around the foot."

"Indeed," Rosario said with a grin. "Maybe we *could* snare those metal monsters."

The only thing that Zoe and Eli could think of was that their dad was on that ship heading for the black hole.

"We've gotta stop them!" Eli insisted.

"You got it!" said Zoe. "That's our target."

"Yeah," said Eli, "but how do we stop them once we catch up to them? How are we gonna take the robots out?"

Terran stepped toward the sphere. "Veda says we must first see them being destroyed in our mind's eye, and believe such a thing is possible."

"Could it be that simple?" Eli asked. "Just *think* it so?"

"Maybe," said Zoe. "It seems fantastic, but so is this whole situation we're in."

"The key," said Walsh, "may be a contrary algorithm. I suggest we explore that angle."

"I admit that the theory is sound," said Mandoon, "but without knowing the mathematical formula or the frequency the robots are on, we wouldn't know how to begin. Even so, I strongly suggest we consider Veda's words. We should all take some time to meditate on the problem. Consider all that we have seen and experienced…, things we cannot explain, and yet they have come to pass. Here we are, streaking through space in this marvelous craft whose control system is a genie, the very personification of the Esseen Crystals themselves. We have no reason to doubt that what Veda has told us is possible. We have only to believe that it is true. Thankfully, we have her to guide us."

Everything was becoming clear now to the space wizard. He could feel the pure understanding of Veda's simple instruction swelling up within him.

"You're right, Commander," Terran said. "Where would we be without Veda? And it seems she never sleeps."

"But *we* do, Captain," said Mandoon. "I suggest we all retire for rest and meditation and then get a fresh start on solving our problems."

"You're right, Mandoon," said Zoe. "As much as I want to rescue Dad, it would be best that we get some sleep while we can."

"I *am* pretty tired," said Eli. "I think we all are."

"Agreed," said Terran. "Everyone get some sleep."

"Eli..., you awake?"

"Yeah. That nap was just what I needed. Man, I feel great!"

"Me, too. I slept like a rock. I thought it would be hard to get to sleep, but I was out as soon as I was down."

As Zoe spoke, he rose from the luxurious body-length pillow he had been sleeping on and proceeded to do a series of deep knee-bends.

"I wonder what Dad is doing and thinking right now," he said.

"He's thinking about us," Eli replied. "I bet things start going our way now. I can feel it."

"Yeah, I feel it, too, bro. Let's get up to the bridge. Come to think of it, I'm pretty hungry."

"Me, too! Man, what about food? Do we have any?"

"I think so. Let's go."

In another part of the ship, Zalcon was just waking up.

"Captain?" he called.

"I'm over here," Terran answered from the alcove in the hallway between their compartments. "How do you feel?"

"I've never slept so soundly, Captain, and I've never felt better."

"Yes," said Terran. "It's the effect the crystals have on us, no doubt."

"Sir, I've been thinking about everything that the genie has said. She believes that we can beat the robots!"

"That was also my impression. We need to hear everything she has to say.... Let's get up there."

As Zoe stepped onto the bridge, he was surprised. "Looks like we're the first ones up this morning..., or afternoon..., or whatever it is.... And the sphere's dark.... Maybe Veda *does* sleep."

At the mention of Veda's name, the opaque sphere filled with white and blue gasses that instantly coalesced into the genie's image. Nodding her head with a tender smile, she said, "*Pace a voi.*"

"Peace to you, too!" Eli and Zoe answered in unison.

Just then, the Maraudian commanders burst onto the bridge, followed by the rest of the crew.

"I'll see to it at once, Captain," Zalcon said. Then, turning to Walsh, he asked, "Do we have any provisions aboard? It's time to eat."

"I'm sorry to report," said Walsh, "that in our haste to get away, we left what little supplies there were on the sea dock."

The crew were now well aware that they were on the verge of starvation as Walsh's words sharpened the pangs of their hunger.

"Okay, so there's no food," said Zoe. "So, what else is new? If I understand Veda, all we have to do is ask.... Our wish is her command..., right?" Then, speaking directly to the sphere, he said, "Veda, we're hungry. Can you help us? A couple of loaves of bread, perhaps?"

Veda smiled. "The universal law of nature will, of course, produce corn for bread, once you have planted the corn seed and passed the time required to grow and harvest it. There is, however, an accelerated version of this law within your own nature, which allows you to bring forth exactly what you need *when* you need it. You have only to realize that this ability to provide exactly what you want is your birthright. First, you must become quiet and visualize what you wish. Then, realizing that you are one with the universal substance that has created you, fill the mold of your desire with your belief, and bring it forth with your spoken word."

Everyone stared at Veda, amazed at the simplicity of her instructions. Her eloquence had brought them to the very threshold of obtaining the keys to the Universe.

Mandoon made the first breakthrough, connecting mere thought with manifestation. "Yes!" he exclaimed. "I see now!" Holding his hands in front of him, palms up, he uttered the words, "Let there be bread!"

To the crew's astonishment, a golden loaf of braided bread appeared in his outstretched hands.

Mandoon repeated the sequence, and another loaf appeared.

"Now *I'll* try," said Terran.

Using Mandoon's exact words, he held out his hands, but nothing happened.

He looked at Mandoon, perplexed. The wizard looked at the genie.

"Captain Terran," Veda said, "you do not yet believe in the power that has already been demonstrated. The flaw is indicated in your words."

"My words?" asked Terran. "I repeated the exact words that

Mandoon spoke..., 'Let there be bread!'"

"Yes," said Veda. "Those *are* the correct words, but they were undermined when you said, 'Let me *try*.' If you absolutely believed, you would not have said 'try.' Total conviction is the key to your success.... But take heart. You have only recently been introduced to your true nature..., your inheritance. You must overcome your previous concepts of false limitation. Only those who are from the Garden and steeped in the powers and influences of the Esseen Crystals possess this facility from early childhood. Of the countless seeds for Gardens of Eden through-out the Universe, there have occasionally been some that were cast on barren ground. Such unfortunate offspring have had to survive without the benefit of the Esseen Crystals. This has been *your* plight. You all come from those lost races that have had to rely on the basic laws of nature to provide for your survival. Consequently, you have convinced yourselves to believe in your own limitations. Before you can inherit your intended estate, you must first cast off this stifling concept of duality..., the idea of separateness between yourself and everything else. In reality, we are all one perfect universal substance that exists eternally in the endless dance of life and unbounded creativity. We are all the one universal creative force called Me. You are but one of the children of the Universe, created in the exact likeness of the Great Mystery. You therefore possess the divine power to create through the spoken word. It is your inheritance. It may require step-by-step practice to break through to the place of knowing that you indeed command the universal substance."

"I see it now," Eli said softly. "This is marvelous!"

Mandoon then brought forth more than enough additional loaves of the delicious, golden brown, crusty bread to satisfy everyone's hunger. He also provided several vessels filled with pure fresh water, after which everyone enjoyed a warm sense of well-being.

Streaking through the Milky Way Galaxy at maximum velocity with the *Maraudor* in tow, the Empire's mother ship once again cut its power and lifted the tractor beam to conduct another routine maintenance call. The robots were oblivious to the puddle they sloshed through as they entered the hangar deck, leaving ultraviolet prints wherever they had been.

Because of the robots' precise, repetitious nature, Chief Mazor and his men were gratified, but not surprised, to see them tread over exactly the same step marks as they had left on their last visit. The prisoners were now ready to put their plan into action. They had two transparent baroulite cables rigged and ready to be placed over the ultraviolet footprints. Mazor and his men would barely have enough time to place the nearly invisible snares and connect them to the pyronite missiles that were hidden halfway between the hatch and the hangar door before the robots were again in position for the trap to be sprung.

As soon as the robots cleared the hangar deck and headed for the bridge, Mazor's men went about stringing the cables out to the missiles that were still in their storage racks, hidden in the shadows under heavy tarps.

Bob and the buccaneers stayed on the bridge with three of the crew so that everything would appear normal when the robots came to perform their tasks. The timing of their brash plan was based on the Illuminosity's predictable routine, which had remained precisely on schedule since the first of now seven maintenance patrols.

Mazor was hiding in the gear locker on the hangar deck, clad in a spacesuit and helmet, waiting to spring the trap that, if successful, would eliminate two of the robots, whose numbers on the mother ship were unknown. At the right moment, he had to raise the hangar door and fire the missiles.

The chance of perfectly coordinating the sequence that was necessary for the missiles to pass without impacting the hangar doors was a long shot at best. Resigned to their own doom, the prisoners all agreed that the risk was worth the devastation that would ensue, should the plan fail. With no desire to reach Ulantia, they were determined to exact as costly a price as possible for their lives.

Chief Mazor clenched a remote control in each hand, one to raise the hangar doors, and the other for the robots' rocket ride, as the hatch rolled open and the first centurion stepped through.

To his shipmates' delight, Mandoon continued to exercise

his newfound creative abilities, providing them with a satisfying repast of the Maraudians' favorite dish—*aubrice*.

After the meal, Terran began to study the sphere's image of the parsec of space they were traveling through. "As far as I can tell," he said, "we should overtake them within two more sleep cycles. Until then, let us continue to explore and understand the power that Mandoon has already demonstrated and that Veda says lies dormant in us all."

As their craft shot through space at incomprehensible speeds, the others aboard the time ship were attempting to obtain the level of mastery that Mandoon had already acquired. Veda continued to impart the consciousness they sought. Her superb eloquence led them into that divine territory of realization that she said was their inheritance.

The next one to achieve the mystifying capabilities was Eli.

"I see now.... I feel it!" With outstretched hands, he said, "Let there be an abundance of apples, grapes, oranges, pineapples, and peaches..., oh, and a watermelon!"

No sooner had the words left his lips, than a cornucopia of his desires appeared next to the water vessels that Mandoon had produced. Then, focusing on one of the vessels of water, Eli said, "Let this be wine!"

When Terran saw the pure water change from clear to ruby red, he was compelled to dip his cup into the vessel and raise it to his lips. Mandoon and his shipmates were astounded to see their captain do this.

"In all of my travels," said Terran, "Never have I tasted anything so divine!"

He quickly finished his sampling and filled his cup again. The Maraudians, who, until this moment would only drink water, now followed their captain's lead and found that they, too, could not resist the wine's charm.

Zoe was next to realize his inheritance. Holding his hands out before him, palms up, he said, "My favorite food with wine is a thin-crust pizza!"

As soon as he uttered these words, a pizza materialized in his hands. It was warmed to perfection with sauce, cheeses, and sausage.

Zoe was beside himself. "It's just what I pictured in my mind's eye and desired with all my heart!"

The Maraudians were ecstatic after tasting what Zoe had brought forth.

Zane spoke for everyone: "Never have I tasted such perfection!"

After Zoe's presentation, Walsh came into his own. The submarine captain manifested a handsome fiddle and bow, which he proceeded to play with obvious familiarity. The atmosphere within the craft was now an intoxicating combination of indulgence and fulfillment as Zalcon and Zane followed Walsh's epiphany, manifesting loaves of bread. Then, realizing they were supplied with food in abundance, Zalcon produced a lute and joined Walsh in making beautiful music. One after another, like popping corn, each Maraudian burst into the divine ability of manifestation. Inspired by the delightful music that Zalcon and

Walsh were playing, the others produced instruments native to their world and joined in. On they went, forgetting the rescue mission for the moment as their creativity followed the dictates of their fancy.

But Terran had yet to manifest anything. While the others carried on, he conferred with Mandoon about what they were experiencing.

"What am I not doing," he asked. "Or what am I doing wrong? Why can I not create as you and the others have done? I have a strong concentrated will to do so."

Recognizing the flaw in Terran's understanding, Mandoon said, "Captain, do not rely on willpower or strong concentrated thought. Your effort must be in the form of sincere desire and absolute conviction that you are one with the universal substance from which all things spring forth. When your belief becomes knowing, you will be free of limitations, free of the idea of duality, and your inheritance will be at hand."

Terran drank Mandoon's words like water. "Thank you, Mandoon, I will meditate further on this."

The music played on, quenching a thirst they had all forgotten. At Zalcon's request, Zoe produced several more pizzas, and Eli brought forth wine to everyone's savor and gratitude. After they had had their fill of the Earthly concoctions, the Maraudians enthusiastically agreed that they were experiencing new horizons of pleasure, not the least of which were those of the palette.

"Captain," said Mandoon, "I don't think I could ever eat

aubrice again."

"Don't even *mention* it again," Terran said with a grimace.

Turning to his captain, Zalcon said, "It would seem that the Lamorians had no qualms about having a woman on board, and now I can understand why. Where would we be without Veda's eloquence and ability to raise us to such a lofty state?" Sipping his wine, he continued, "Captain, remember back on Rosario's ship, that beautiful woman who wanted to come with us?"

Terran grinned, also sipping Eli's wine. "Yes, Commander, I remember her saying she wanted to accompany *me*."

Zalcon laughed at Terran's meaning. "Yes, Captain. Yes, you are correct in your recollection. But maybe having a woman on board *would* be something to consider in the future..., perhaps even a *crew* of women."

The eruption of laughter was contagious. Even Mandoon cackled as everyone agreed with Zalcon's notions. The cosmic party might have continued well past the Sagittarius Constellation had Veda not made an announcement: "We are about to overtake the Illuminosity's mother ship and its hostages."

The two centurions marched onto the hangar deck as the interior hatch slid shut behind them. They were oblivious to the presence of Chief Mazor, who was watching through the crack of the gear locker doors, waiting to detonate the booby traps that were conceived out of sheer desperation. His right hand tightened its grip on the remote that would open the great doors, exposing the hangar to the infinite sea of space. He could only hope they would open in time to allow the pyronite missiles to pass through.

If Mazor's plan succeeded, he and his men would rush aboard the sky barge as soon as the hangar doors were shut to attempt to land back on the Illuminosity's ship and detonate another rack of pyronite missiles. Certain that this would be a one-way mission, the Maraudians consoled themselves that they would be exacting an exorbitant price for their lives.

The moment was at hand. The robots were standing in precisely the anticipated spot in front of the docking collar. When Mazor pressed the first remote, the space door responded instantly. He immediately pressed the second remote, but there was no response. As the hangar deck depressurized, the two robots paused to calculate the unexpected event. Realizing the failure of the remote, Mazor burst out of the gear locker. Repeatedly pressing the remote in his outstretched hand while moving as fast as he could in his magnetic boots, he went bounding toward the rack of missiles hidden in the shadows. This was his only chance for success. He was midway across the hangar deck when the signal finally reached through the heavy cover and lit up the shadows in a fiery explosion, sending the missiles on their way amid smoke and blazing tarps.

As the rockets cleared the hangar, the two baroulite nooses snapped around the robots' feet and swept them out on their backs toward the open hatch. Mazor was caught standing in the middle of this confusion. The first robot barely missed him as it slid by. The second came careening into the chief, grabbing him in its claw-like grip as he toppled. The two were whisked away, disappearing into the endless night.

Unaware of the tragic success of the first phase of the plan, Mazor's men waited for the lights on their side of the hatch to indicate that the space door was closed and the compartment was repressurized. Instead, to their chagrin, they heard the sound of the sky barge lifting off, followed by the jarring shift in the ship's inertia, signaling the reactivation of the tractor beam.

When the crew heard Veda's announcement, their jovial mood quickly changed to sober-minded determination.

"The robots will be coming into range," Terran said. "We need a plan *now!*"

"Before we can rescue my father and the others," Eli said, "we must disengage the Illuminosity's hold on the *Maraudor.*"

"That's easier said than done," Zalcon answered. "We will have to board their ship and neutralize the robots in order to seize the controls and recover the crystals. And let's face it…. Unless we can catch them with their hangar doors open, gaining entry may prove problematic."

"Problematic hardly seems an appropriate term," Terran said with a grin, "from one who manifests his own musical instruments out of thin air."

Zalcon smiled in tacit acknowledgment.

"Veda," Zoe asked, "what must we do to rescue my father and the others?"

"These machines," Veda said, "are not of the one spiritual body called *Me*. Although they seem impregnable, ultimately they consist of the universal substance, which is subject to your desires and will. The universal substance responds to the *I am* of reality. Thus, you have but to visualize what you desire and bring it forth as before, with your spoken word. Go forth and overcome the negativity in this way. Retrieve those who are dear to us and then proceed on to all that is good."

Once again, Veda's simple instruction directed their focus to their divine inheritance.

"Yeah!" said Walsh. "We could visualize in our mind's eye a torpedo or missile that would penetrate their ship with a contrary algorithm and scramble their central control system."

A torpedo was a concept the old submarine captain was familiar with, so he could easily form its image in his mind.

"Perhaps," said Mandoon, "such a missile could do what must be done. But I think there is a simpler solution. Rather than bringing forth a weapon, we could simply appeal to the Great Mystery to accomplish our goal in a way that is better than we can imagine. That would free us from the limitations of specifics. We should all become quiet and meditate, focusing on our sincere desire. Once we have this concept firmly in mind, each of us must make the affirmation, 'Let this entanglement work out better than we could have ever imagined.'"

"Thank you, Commander," said Terran. "I agree. Let us all use the remaining time before our confrontation with the Illuminosity to follow Mandoon's advice."

As the chamber fell into silent meditation, there arose what sounded like a choir resonating a single note—softly at first, then steadily building in volume to embrace the full spectrum of a harmonious *OMMMMM.*

Shortly after the robots left the bridge, Bob, Rosario, and Knox had joined the others, who were waiting by the hatch for the safety lights that would be their signal to rush the hangar deck.

"Forget about it," Bob said. "Those lights aren't coming back on."

"Aye, to be sure," said Knox. "We all know the sound of that sky barge when it gets under way. Our man must be dead in there, and the robots 'ave left the ship.... So now what?"

"That's not hard to figure," Bob said. "There are two possibilities. Either the snares took out their targets, and there was a third robot waiting on board the sky barge..., or the snares missed, and Mazor was swept out into space or taken back to the mother ship. The bottom line is we've failed, and now they're onto us."

"Aye," said Knox. "And they'll be back to settle the score, to be sure."

Rosario's wide-eyed glare was more accentuated than ever. "You're right, Mister Knox. I'm afraid all we have done is to seal our fate."

"No doubt," Assistant Chief Tamlok concurred. "Now the robots will be compelled to terminate us. They always make an example of anyone who resists."

"We have no weapons," said Rosario. "We can't even go out fighting. All we can do is wait here to be slaughtered like so many chickens."

The despair in his voice was contagious.

Trying to shore up the men's plummeting confidence, Tamlok said, "If we can get to the pyronite missiles and detonate them, we may be close enough to disable their ship so they can never make it back to Ulantia."

But then, remembering that the hangar door was still open, and anyone entering the hangar deck would be sucked out into space, Tamlok grimaced. At the same moment, everyone else realized the obvious flaw in his statement: they could *never* get to the missiles.

The centurion who was piloting the sky barge reported the elimination of the two robots and the human almost as it happened. By the time the sky barge landed on the mother ship, the high command had already calculated its response and was ready to retaliate. The shuttle pilot was joined by three more centurions, who carried the repellite chests containing the crystals. The robots had originally planned to deposit the Esseen Crystals into the irretrievable abyss of the black hole. Considering this most recent incident, they decided to dispose of the humans and their ship as well. A relatively short distance remained to what would be the point of no return for the *Maraudor* and the hostages.

As the sky barge started back to the *Maraudor*, the Lamorian time ship suddenly appeared on the Illuminosity's screen.

While the hypnotic *OMMMMM* continued to reverberate throughout the craft, Veda explained that this was the sound of their own ship's weaponry.

"Everyone look here," Terran said, pointing at the sphere.

They could see that the Illuminosity's ship, with the *Maraudor* in tow, was rapidly approaching the influences of the black hole, and that the sky barge was returning to the *Maraudor*.

"Head for that sky barge!" Terran ordered.

As the time ship complied, the sky barge came around to align itself with the intruder.

Veda's voice rose above the background drone: "The Esseen Crystals are aboard the approaching craft."

As she spoke, the sky barge unleashed a full spread of pyronite missiles, all of which appeared to be on target. Terran was well aware of pyronite's unique ability to penetrate the repellite hull of the time ship.

"Everyone, brace for impact!" he called out. But then, realizing the negative nature of the command, he said, "Belay that order! I believe this will turn out better than we could have imagined!"

No sooner had he spoken than the missiles slammed into the golden aurora of the time ship's force field, causing a horrendous explosion. But the time ship remained unscathed.

Realizing the magnitude of the detonation they had just withstood invigorated everyone.

Terran instinctively gave the order, "Return fire!"

To everyone's astonishment, the time ship responded immediately, issuing a concentrated plasmic charge that engulfed the sky barge, fusing its systems and occupants.

A wave of relief swept over the crew as they watched these events unfolding within the sphere.

"Veda, what happened?" asked Zoe. "Are they still alive?"

"They were never alive," she replied. "By your command, all the machines aboard the craft have been permanently neutralized. The Esseen Crystals, however, are intact."

"Better than we could have imagined," Terran said reverently.

"Captain," said Mandoon, "you have saved us all with your understanding of the principles of your innate power. Congratulations!"

Acknowledging Mandoon with a quick nod, Terran ordered, "Close on the sky barge! We must retrieve the crystals before we can continue the chase."

"But, Captain," objected Zoe, "we may not have enough time to do both!"

"Yes, Captain," said Eli, "we must save the others first!"

Terran remained firm in his priorities. "Stay on course," he said. "The crystals are essential to all of mankind. We must save them at *all* cost. Trust me on this. I believe things will work out for everyone better than we can imagine."

Veda's face reappeared in the sphere. "Captain Terran is correct," she said.

As her image dissolved, they could see in the sphere that they were about to connect with the sky barge.

"Zalcon," said Terran, "take four men and prepare to board."

"At once, Captain!" Zalcon replied. Pointing to four of the crew, he said, "You're with me. Let's go."

There was only silence when Zalcon's boarding party entered the bridge of the sky barge.

"It's just as Veda described, Captain," Zalcon said into his headset. "The four robots are still in their seats, fused solid. I never thought I would see these once invincible robots reduced to useless hulks of scrap. And the sky barge…, it cannot be salvaged."

"Understood," said Terran. "Secure the crystals and get back here!"

"There they are," Zalcon said, pointing to the three familiar chests with their precious contents.

Minutes later, Zalcon and his men were back aboard the time ship, which then took off in hot pursuit. Terran and his officers were delighted that they finally had a ship and weaponry capable of defeating the nefarious Empire. But for now, they had to put off their exuberance, since there was still much to do and the robots were on the run.

The Empire's mother ship and the *Marauder* had been jostled by the plasmic wave that neutralized the sky barge and its crew, but were otherwise unharmed by the rapidly dissipating charge. Realizing they were up against superior weaponry, the robots accelerated the mother ship to maximum velocity toward the edge of the black hole.

Everyone aboard the time ship watched the sphere anxiously as it showed them closing in on the mother ship and the *Maraudor*.

"Not good," said Terran. "They have arrived at the event horizon."

"What do you mean?" asked Zoe.

"What's the event horizon?" asked Eli.

"It is the point," explained Mandoon, "beyond which you cannot escape the gravitational pull of the cosmic abyss."

The brothers' hearts sank in despair.

"We shouldn't have gone after the sky barge!" Eli railed bitterly. "We could have stopped them in time!"

"This is turning out to be *worse* than we could have imagined," Zoe ranted.

"Steady, boys," said Walsh, consolingly. "Remember, it ain't over till it's over. Consider everything we have accomplished, and don't lose sight of what Veda has taught us."

The crew watched in horror as the mother ship cut its tractor beam and veered off toward the edge of the galaxy, hurling the *Maraudor* and its luckless passengers into the unfathomable depths of the black hole.

Without a moment's hesitation, Terran said, "We're too late. Make for the mother ship! We can and will overtake the robots long before they make it to Ulantia. We will neutralize that mother ship and then go on to Ulantia and do the same to the central control of the Empire. We will envision their termination coming about more quickly and easily than anyone could have imagined, and we will make it so as soon as we arrive there. We will then go on to vanquish the Empire's hold on the many worlds of our galaxy and restore them to gardens of enlightenment."

Everyone embraced Terran's heroic plan except Eli and Zoe.

"No, Captain!" Zoe pleaded. "You can't! We *must* save my father and your crew."

"That's right, Captain!" Eli cried. "We can use our powers to make it so. We *must!*"

In the midst of all this, Veda's image appeared in the sphere.

"The *Maraudor* and those aboard her have passed beyond the point of no return," she said. "The gravity of the abyss is so vast that nothing as infinitesimal as the *Maraudor* could ever escape its influence."

"Any closer," said Terran, "and we would be in the same predicament."

Zoe was crushed. "So much for things turning out better than we could imagine."

"Take heart, Zoroaster," Veda said, looking deep into Zoe's tearful eyes. "These events do not contradict your affirmations.

There is a way."

Hugging his brother, Eli said, "Of course! Veda has never steered us wrong! There *must* be a way!"

"Captain Terran," said Veda, pointing to the circular column that was the core of the time ship, "please return the crystals to their chamber, the Middle of the Middle."

Terran opened the first of the three chests and lifted out one of the crystals. Holding it like an infant in his arms, he said, "This is the most sacred and precious object in the Universe."

The men huddled closer, sharing the ecstasy of the moment. Then, one by one, each man came up to touch the crystal. Finally, Terran placed it into one of the nine empty receptacles within the chamber.

Mandoon took the second crystal and placed it in the chamber, followed by Zalcon, who did the same with the third. This went on until every man, some in pairs, had a chance to place a crystal.

As soon as the ninth crystal was put in place, the chamber lit up with a sparkling golden luminescence.

"It is done," said Veda.

"Eli!" Zoe cried out. "Remember back on that island, when Shakti took us into a chamber just like this one? She called it the Middle of the Middle, too."

"Yeah, I remember…. You know, I have a feeling that this is just a dark corner in the turn of events that *will* work out better than we can imagine."

Zoe found new confidence in Eli's words. "Right," he said.

"I believe that. But what happens now? Dad is dead and we are eons from home in pursuit of those robots, involved in a cause that's not our own."

"We are all the One called Me," said Veda. "It is now as it has always been. All things are woven into the cosmic fabric of perfection. All things are possible. You have but to desire what awaits you."

"In other words," said Zoe, "we have to enter the chamber, just like we did before with Shakti, and let the crystals put it all back together for us again."

Veda smiled. "Go forth and rejoin those you have left behind. Just as the Maraudians must return to free the peoples of *their* world, so must you and your brother return to *your* rightful place in the Universe. Perfection is always one step ahead as it beckons to us."

As always, Veda's eloquence made everything clear. Terran and his mates were eager to return to their world as saviors. The Esseen Crystals and the Lamorian time ship were all they needed to bring down the Illuminosity.

"Veda," said Mandoon, "how long will it take us to reach Marauda?"

"Sooner than you can imagine," she said.

"I thrive on adventure," said Walsh. "I have no desire to go back to Earth. I wish to go on with you, Captain Terran, and to whatever destiny awaits us."

"Yes," said Terran, we are alike in our thirst for adventure. It would be an honor to have you join us, Captain Walsh. Perhaps after we have liberated our people from the Empire, we can bring the crystals back to your people on Earth."

The brothers knew what they had to do. The crystals would return them to a time before they left, creating a new version of their reality. Right now, under the influence of the crystals, they knew all that had occurred back on the island when this fantastic adventure began.

"So that's it, then," said Eli.

"Yeah," Zoe said. "We're all done here. Let's get going."

"You realize that we won't remember any of this. It's a shame to have been on this unbelievable adventure and have no recollection of it or this fabulous inheritance."

"I know. But at least we won't have to remember losing Dad. The inheritance will always be there, waiting for us to redis-cover it. Let's go!"

It was time for the brothers to say farewell to their mates.

"We will be leaving you all now," Eli said. "Captain, I wish we could tell you that we will never forget what we have had together here, but I'm afraid the opposite is the case."

"Understood," said Terran. "We could never have accomplished all of this without you. We will never forget you two, and I am confident that we will meet again."

The brothers started for the central chamber amid warm farewells and affectionate smiles from the crew.

Veda's last words to them made the scene perfect: "One thing that remains, regardless of memory, is that we are all cosmic raindrops falling to the sea, and when we arrive, we will be

Me.... We are *all* the One called Me. We shall all meet again."

As Eli and Zoe entered the Middle of the Middle, they were engulfed in sparkling particles of golden amber and silver. They felt a swirling sensation of euphoria as the sounds of chimes solidified into the realization that their doorbell was ringing.

Bob was in the kitchen, reading the morning newspaper. There was a story on the front page about a tragedy in the North Atlantic. A Captain Walsh and his crew of the elite *Trieste III* had been lost at sea.

Eli peered through the window before answering the door.

"It's FedEx," he said. Opening the door, he signed for a large envelope.

"What is it?" Zoe asked anxiously.

They had been hoping to hear something about their deep-sea discovery that was now in the hands of Dr. Abblett, the U.S. chief oceanographer.

As Eli tore open the envelope, Bob went back to the article he was reading. "I wonder," he said, "if that Captain Walsh was involved with the search for our UFO?"

"Maybe so," Zoe said. "It was a deep-sea research vehicle, wasn't it?"

But his question suddenly became irrelevant as Eli dumped the contents of the envelope out onto the kitchen table.

"Man, look at *this!*"

The photos of their undersea discovery and the dossier of Dr. Dave's findings were being returned. Eli read aloud the enclosed letter, whose last words were:

> After an extensive search effort and subsequent
> loss of life and equipment, it is the decision of
> this department that the UFO has either left the
> area or, due to turbulent dispersion, is otherwise
> irretrievable. The search is hereby terminated.

"How do you like that?" Eli said. "And it's signed by Dr. Brendan Abblett of the U.S. Oceanographic Institute."

"Well, that's it," was Bob's only comment.

With a feeling of relief, Eli said, "Now we can get back to our lives and forget about UFOs."

Zoe agreed, surprised himself that he was so willing to drop the whole matter.

"Yeah," he said, "now we can get our heads back in the game..., *our* game at Paintball Jungle!"

www.ingramcontent.com/pod-product-compliance
Lightning Source LLC
Chambersburg PA
CBHW030529020726
47494CB00004B/1280